The New York Times

IN THE HEADLINES

Restorative Justice

AN ALTERNATIVE TO PUNISHMENT

THE NEW YORK TIMES EDITORIAL STAFF

Published in 2021 by New York Times Educational Publishing
in association with The Rosen Publishing Group, Inc.
29 East 21st Street, New York, NY 10010

First Edition

The New York Times
Caroline Que: Editorial Director, Book Development
Cecilia Bohan: Photo Rights/Permissions Editor
Heidi Giovine: Administrative Manager

Rosen Publishing
Megan Kellerman: Managing Editor
Michael Hessel-Mial: Editor
Brian Garvey: Art Director

Cataloging-in-Publication Data
Names: New York Times Company.
Title: Restorative justice: an alternative to punishment / edited by
the New York Times editorial staff.
Description: New York : New York Times Educational Publishing,
2021. | Series: In the headlines | Includes glossary and index.
Identifiers: ISBN 9781642824155 (library bound) | ISBN
9781642824148 (pbk.) | ISBN 9781642824162 (ebook)
Subjects: LCSH: Restorative justice—United States. |
Discrimination in criminal justice administration—United States. |
Anti-racism—United States. | Race awareness—United States.
Classification: LCC HV8688.R478 2021 |
DDC 320.97301'1—dc23

Manufactured in the United States of America

On the cover: Educators and administrators take part in a
restorative justice training session at Lakeview Elementary School
auditorium on March 14, 2013, in Oakland, Calif.; Ann Hermes/
The Christian Science Monitor/Getty Images.

Contents

CHAPTER 3

Community Voices: Unrest, Innovation, Involvement

Introduction

GOVERNMENTS FROM THE local to national level do a great many things, but one common feature of them all is the authority to use force. Individual citizens cannot possess nuclear weapons or imprison people; only a governing authority is granted that right. Democratic societies are designed, moreover, to give ordinary citizens some degree of a voice in how that right to use force is used. Democracies are premised on the idea that the people ultimately decide — although often in an indirect way — how and whether a government may restrain, punish or kill.

It's a serious responsibility. Our laws decide what kinds of behaviors are considered crimes, which crimes deserve harsh punishments and which crimes deserve leniency. Those laws have tended to change with our social values. We look back at some old laws with puzzlement, as in a New Jersey law requiring all horses to wear sleigh bells, and disappointment, as in laws banning interracial marriage. The sillier laws reflect some long-past public interest, and the oppressive laws remind us whose needs were neglected.

Future generations may look back at America's legal system with puzzlement and disappointment. Since the 1970s, when President Richard Nixon expanded federal funds for policing, and the 1980s, when President Ronald Reagan launched the first of several "tough on crime" laws, American criminal justice has been characterized by heavily militarized policing and harsh punishments for crimes. Today, the United States has the highest incarceration rate in the world. It also has more killings by police officers than those in Mexico, Pakistan, Argentina or Egypt. And Americans aren't necessarily safer for it. While the United States did experience a crime wave that prompted this initial incarceration and policing boom, criminologists disagree whether these punitive measures had any effect on our long-dropping crime rate.

In response to both protests and resource constraints, there is increasing talk of criminal justice reform. But what should that reform look like? One model gaining traction is known as "restorative justice." This approach is premised on a redefinition of crime: An offense is not committed by a "bad guy" in need of "punishment," but instead is a harm to the community in need of healing. Restorative justice centers around dialogue between the victim and offender, to allow the offender to understand the harm and make efforts to repair it. On a deeper level, it entails community involvement in social health as a way to build the social ties that make people less likely to hurt one another. Though restorative justice was first pioneered in the United States in the 1970s, it has long-established precedents in indigenous societies. Some of the practices described in this book, for example, were established by Māori people in New Zealand centuries ago.

Some practitioners of restorative justice are community leaders, and some are criminal justice researchers. Still others are activists with a more controversial platform: the abolition of prisons and police altogether. Their argument is based on the following claim: that many criminal justice institutions had their origins in suppressing minority populations and the enduring remnants of such oppression live on under the supposed neutrality of the law. For abolitionists, prisons and policing are incorrect responses to problems with solutions elsewhere: in the realms of mental health, environmental protections, anti-poverty programs and housing. Abolitionists often note that the United States increased spending on prisons and policing at the same time that it cut similar spending for social welfare. As you read the articles in this title, you will have the opportunity to think through these arguments. You'll also find that abolitionist writers Michelle Alexander and Ruth Wilson Gilmore do not pretend violence doesn't exist. Rather, these authors offer a rich, compassionate view of how to stop it, and how to begin the process of social healing in

Betsye Steele, a high school principal, speaks with a student during a restorative justice session. Many schools are turning to such formal, trust-building dialogues as an alternative to school suspensions.

troubled communities. Restorative justice is often a critical tool in this alternative approach to dealing with violence.

As of 2020, criminal justice reform is gaining momentum, but it's unclear what the priorities of that reform will be. A number of contending views — conservative, liberal, reactionary, radical, moderate — are scrambling to influence the direction such reform will take. Will we tweak the system with police body cameras and new prisoner resources? Will we release a few thousand offenders or really cut our prison population? Will the hard-line prison abolitionists win? Will we make our harsh laws still harsher? Or will we do nothing? Any one of these things could happen, and each of them could make a substantial difference in people's lives inside and outside the home, community or prison. The fundamental question of restorative justice is: What do communities need to be healthy and safe?

CHAPTER 1

The Mass Incarceration Puzzle

The American criminal justice system has two contradictory features. First: America has the highest incarceration rate in the world, holding close to a quarter of the world's prisoners. Second: Crime has been falling somewhat independently of imprisonment. The American system is characterized by: harsher sentences than in other developed nations, high racial disparities in who does and doesn't get locked up, and a disturbing tendency to trap prisoners and their families in poverty.

U.S. Prison Population Dwarfs That of Other Nations

BY ADAM LIPTAK | APRIL 23, 2008

THE UNITED STATES has less than 5 percent of the world's population. But it has almost a quarter of the world's prisoners.

Indeed, the United States leads the world in producing prisoners, a reflection of a relatively recent and now entirely distinctive American approach to crime and punishment. Americans are locked up for crimes — from writing bad checks to using drugs — that would rarely produce prison sentences in other countries. And in particular they are kept incarcerated far longer than prisoners in other nations.

Criminologists and legal scholars in other industrialized nations say they are mystified and appalled by the number and length of American prison sentences.

The United States has, for instance, 2.3 million criminals behind bars, more than any other nation, according to data maintained by the International Center for Prison Studies at King's College London.

China, which is four times more populous than the United States, is a distant second, with 1.6 million people in prison. (That number excludes hundreds of thousands of people held in administrative detention, most of them in China's extrajudicial system of re-education through labor, which often singles out political activists who have not committed crimes.)

San Marino, with a population of about 30,000, is at the end of the long list of 218 countries compiled by the center. It has a single prisoner.

The United States comes in first, too, on a more meaningful list from the prison studies center, the one ranked in order of the incarceration rates. It has 751 people in prison or jail for every 100,000 in population. (If you count only adults, one in 100 Americans is locked up.)

The only other major industrialized nation that even comes close is Russia, with 627 prisoners for every 100,000 people. The others have much lower rates. England's rate is 151; Germany's is 88; and Japan's is 63.

The median among all nations is about 125, roughly a sixth of the American rate.

There is little question that the high incarceration rate here has helped drive down crime, though there is debate about how much.

Criminologists and legal experts here and abroad point to a tangle of factors to explain America's extraordinary incarceration rate: higher levels of violent crime, harsher sentencing laws, a legacy of racial turmoil, a special fervor in combating illegal drugs, the American temperament, and the lack of a social safety net. Even democracy plays a role, as judges — many of whom are elected, another American anomaly — yield to populist demands for tough justice.

Whatever the reason, the gap between American justice and that of the rest of the world is enormous and growing.

It used to be that Europeans came to the United States to study its prison systems. They came away impressed.

"In no country is criminal justice administered with more mildness than in the United States," Alexis de Tocqueville, who toured American penitentiaries in 1831, wrote in "Democracy in America."

No more.

"Far from serving as a model for the world, contemporary America is viewed with horror," James Whitman, a specialist in comparative law at Yale, wrote last year in Social Research. "Certainly there are no European governments sending delegations to learn from us about how to manage prisons."

Prison sentences here have become "vastly harsher than in any other country to which the United States would ordinarily be compared," Michael Tonry, a leading authority on crime policy, wrote in "The Handbook of Crime and Punishment."

Indeed, said Vivien Stern, a research fellow at the prison studies center in London, the American incarceration rate has made the United States "a rogue state, a country that has made a decision not to follow what is a normal Western approach."

The spike in American incarceration rates is quite recent. From 1925 to 1975, the rate remained stable, around 110 people in prison per 100,000 people. It shot up with the movement to get tough on crime in the late 1970s. (These numbers exclude people held in jails, as comprehensive information on prisoners held in state and local jails was not collected until relatively recently.)

The nation's relatively high violent crime rate, partly driven by the much easier availability of guns here, helps explain the number of people in American prisons.

"The assault rate in New York and London is not that much different," said Marc Mauer, the executive director of the Sentencing Project, a research and advocacy group. "But if you look at the murder rate, particularly with firearms, it's much higher."

Despite the recent decline in the murder rate in the United States, it is still about four times that of many nations in Western Europe.

But that is only a partial explanation. The United States, in fact, has relatively low rates of nonviolent crime. It has lower burglary and robbery rates than Australia, Canada and England.

People who commit nonviolent crimes in the rest of the world are less likely to receive prison time and certainly less likely to receive long sentences. The United States is, for instance, the only advanced country that incarcerates people for minor property crimes like passing bad checks, Whitman wrote.

Efforts to combat illegal drugs play a major role in explaining long prison sentences in the United States as well. In 1980, there were about 40,000 people in American jails and prisons for drug crimes. These days, there are almost 500,000.

Those figures have drawn contempt from European critics. "The U.S. pursues the war on drugs with an ignorant fanaticism," said Stern of King's College.

Many American prosecutors, on the other hand, say that locking up people involved in the drug trade is imperative, as it helps thwart demand for illegal drugs and drives down other kinds of crime. Attorney General Michael Mukasey, for instance, has fought hard to prevent the early release of people in federal prison on crack cocaine offenses, saying that many of them "are among the most serious and violent offenders."

Still, it is the length of sentences that truly distinguishes American prison policy. Indeed, the mere number of sentences imposed here would not place the United States at the top of the incarceration lists. If lists were compiled based on annual admissions to prison per capita, several European countries would outpace the United States. But American prison stays are much longer, so the total incarceration rate is higher.

Burglars in the United States serve an average of 16 months in prison, according to Mauer, compared with 5 months in Canada and 7 months in England.

Many specialists dismissed race as an important distinguishing factor in the American prison rate. It is true that blacks are much more likely to be imprisoned than other groups in the United States, but that is not a particularly distinctive phenomenon. Minorities in Canada, Britain and Australia are also disproportionately represented in those nations' prisons, and the ratios are similar to or larger than those in the United States.

Some scholars have found that English-speaking nations have higher prison rates.

"Although it is not at all clear what it is about Anglo-Saxon culture that makes predominantly English-speaking countries especially punitive, they are," Tonry wrote last year in "Crime, Punishment and Politics in Comparative Perspective."

"It could be related to economies that are more capitalistic and political cultures that are less social democratic than those of most European countries," Tonry wrote. "Or it could have something to do with the Protestant religions with strong Calvinist overtones that were long influential."

The American character — self-reliant, independent, judgmental — also plays a role.

"America is a comparatively tough place, which puts a strong emphasis on individual responsibility," Whitman of Yale wrote. "That attitude has shown up in the American criminal justice of the last 30 years."

French-speaking countries, by contrast, have "comparatively mild penal policies," Tonry wrote.

Of course, sentencing policies within the United States are not monolithic, and national comparisons can be misleading.

"Minnesota looks more like Sweden than like Texas," said Mauer of the Sentencing Project. (Sweden imprisons about 80 people per 100,000 of population; Minnesota, about 300; and Texas, almost 1,000. Maine has the lowest incarceration rate in the United States, at 273; and Louisiana the highest, at 1,138.)

Whatever the reasons, there is little dispute that America's exceptional incarceration rate has had an impact on crime.

"As one might expect, a good case can be made that fewer Americans are now being victimized" thanks to the tougher crime policies, Paul Cassell, an authority on sentencing and a former federal judge, wrote in The Stanford Law Review.

From 1981 to 1996, according to Justice Department statistics, the risk of punishment rose in the United States and fell in England. The crime rates predictably moved in the opposite directions, falling in the United States and rising in England.

"These figures," Cassell wrote, "should give one pause before too quickly concluding that European sentences are appropriate."

Other commentators were more definitive. "The simple truth is that imprisonment works," wrote Kent Scheidegger and Michael Rushford of the Criminal Justice Legal Foundation in The Stanford Law and Policy Review. "Locking up criminals for longer periods reduces the level of crime. The benefits of doing so far offset the costs."

There is a counterexample, however, to the north. "Rises and falls in Canada's crime rate have closely paralleled America's for 40 years," Tonry wrote last year. "But its imprisonment rate has remained stable."

Several specialists here and abroad pointed to a surprising explanation for the high incarceration rate in the United States: democracy.

Most state court judges and prosecutors in the United States are elected and are therefore sensitive to a public that is, according to opinion polls, generally in favor of tough crime policies. In the rest of the world, criminal justice professionals tend to be civil servants who are insulated from popular demands for tough sentencing.

Whitman, who has studied Tocqueville's work on American penitentiaries, was asked what accounted for America's booming prison population.

"Unfortunately, a lot of the answer is democracy — just what Tocqueville was talking about," he said. "We have a highly politicized criminal justice system."

The Real Murder Mystery? It's the Low Crime Rate

OPINION | BY SHAILA DEWAN | AUG. 1, 2009

MAYBE IT IS TIME to call in one of those clairvoyants who help detectives solve the case. Because no one else can explain what criminals have been doing in the first half of 2009.

Not that the news is bad — from New York to Los Angeles to Madison, Wis., major crimes, violent or not, are down between 7 percent and 22 percent over the same period last year. In Chicago, the number of homicides dropped 12 percent. In Charlotte, N.C., hard hit by the banking crisis, that total fell an astounding 38 percent. It is too soon to conclude that crime will decline throughout the recession, and the new numbers, which come from standardized reports that police departments send to the F.B.I., have yet to be made into a national measure. But crime was supposed to go up, not sharply down.

The surprise is yet more proof that tea leaves and sun spots may be a better predictor of crime rates than criminologists and the police. Despite the large sums the country spends on law enforcement — just last week, the Justice Department awarded the first of $1 billion in stimulus-package grants to police departments — experts are largely at a loss to explain what makes the crime rate go up or down. Even the exceptions to the latest trend are baffling. Why, for example, did crime go up in Denver, of all places? Denver isn't sure.

Many experienced criminologists admit to being confounded, but point out that economists have no better track record. "If I could predict the crime rate," said Barry Krisberg, the president of the National Council on Crime and Delinquency, "I'd start working as a stock broker."

No single lens — sociological, econometrical, liberal or conservative — seems an adequate one through which to view crime. The economy, which seems as if it should be fundamental, has never been a good predictor; the Prohibition era was far more violent than the Great Depression. Adding prison beds has not helped; the incarceration rate has marched grimly upward for decades, while the crime rate has zigzagged up and down, seemingly oblivious. Years ago, criminologists thought demographics explained a lot — remember the warnings about thousands of cold-blooded, teenage "superpredators" in the mid-1990s? — but demographics cannot shed light on what is happening now. Improved policing deserves credit for bigger declines in certain cities, but not the overall national trend.

Scholars have attributed lower crime rates to everything from an influx of immigrants, who tend to keep a low profile; to changes in public housing policy that have dispersed the poor; to better medicine (more lives saved in the operating room equals fewer homicides); to a marked shift in the attitudes of the young and poor (the hip-hop generation, which was supposed to be desensitized by explicit lyrics and large swaths of visible underwear, has turned out fine).

The search for a silver bullet — a single factor that could explain the steady drop in crime since the mid-1990s — has taken theorists far afield. There is the abortion theory, which proposes that legalized abortion reduced the number of unwanted children who turned to a life of crime. It's a seductive explanation for United States data, but it does not bear out in other countries that legalized abortion in the 1970s, said Franklin E. Zimring, a law professor at the University of California at Berkeley. There is the gun theory, which posits that expanded gun ownership rights have deterred criminals who now must consider whether their victims are armed. But that does not explain the most significant decline in the country, in New York City, where gun ownership is low, said Mr. Zimring, who dedicated part of his book, "The Great American Crime Decline," to debunking such theories. (Despite writing that exhaustive volume, Professor Zimring admits that for criminologists, "the score is Know: 2; Don't Know: 8.")

Even mainstream theories can falter under scrutiny. The idea that illegal drug use drives up crime is not bolstered by statistics that show that the percentage of those arrested in New York City with illegal drugs in their system has remained more or less flat, Mr. Zimring said.

One reason for the lack of answers is lack of money, said Alfred Blumstein, a prominent criminologist at Carnegie Mellon University in Pittsburgh. "The National Institutes of Health spends $400 million a year on dental research," he said. "The National Institute of Justice spends $50 million a year on criminal justice research."

Perhaps as a result, police departments and prosecutors can be swayed by fads, spending millions on programs like Drug Abuse Resistance Education, or D.A.R.E., which came under fire from critics who said it lacked a proven success record (it later changed its strategy). "Police research is to research like military music is to music," Mr. Krisberg said. "It has never matured to be a very sophisticated science."

For the police, of course, crime policy is a political matter, with new theories attracting new money. In 2006, when violent crime inched up by less than 2 percentage points, the Police Executive Research Forum issued a report called "A Gathering Storm."

But the police were not the only ones who thought crime could not stay at post-1960 lows. The thugs and marauders were supposed to be back with a vengeance after the horrors of crack cocaine receded from memory; the safety net was dismantled; and education reform proved slow.

Last year, The Third Way, a progressive think tank, gathered governors like Kathleen Sebelius of Kansas, now President Obama's secretary of Health and Human Services, and Janet Napolitano of Arizona, now secretary of Homeland Security, to warn of "the impending crime wave," identifying such factors as "the lengthening shadow of illegal immigration" and "the sprawling parentless neighborhood of the Internet."

Such appeals to Americans' fears, several criminologists said, is often linked to a political agenda fueled less by crime than by another variable that is famously unfazed by real-world predictors: public perception. Along with its report, The Third Way released a poll showing that by a 5-to-1 ratio, Americans believed crime was worse than it had been the year before. By year's end, though, the national crime data showed a decrease. In Atlanta, where crime is down 10 percent, a recent series of high-profile incidents has spurred critics to hammer the mayor over what they call a crisis.

While the decline may not have taken hold in the minds of the public, it has undermined a cherished belief, particularly among liberals, in root causes — that criminals are born of misery and the limited options of poverty. "There are people that are putting up with an awful lot of suffering, and they're not complaining all that much," said Andrew Karmen, a criminologist at the John Jay College of Criminal Justice in New York.

But the fact that so few forces have a demonstrable effect on crime can be viewed, in a twisted kind of way, as good news. The decline, Mr. Zimring said, has shown that it isn't necessary to accomplish major feats, like improving education or raising wages, or punitive ones, like increasing prison sentences, to bring crime down. Smart policing can have an effect. "Crime isn't an essential part of cities as we know them," Mr. Zimring said. Instead, it is a mystery with a direction all its own, one that may be beyond the reach of public policy. Which is easier to tolerate when that direction is down.

SHAILA DEWAN is a national reporter and editor covering criminal justice issues including prosecution, policing and incarceration.

Prison and the Poverty Trap

BY JOHN TIERNEY | FEB. 18, 2013

WASHINGTON — Why are so many American families trapped in poverty? Of all the explanations offered by Washington's politicians and economists, one seems particularly obvious in the low-income neighborhoods near the Capitol: because there are so many parents like Carl Harris and Charlene Hamilton.

For most of their daughters' childhood, Mr. Harris didn't come close to making the minimum wage. His most lucrative job, as a crack dealer, ended at the age of 24, when he left Washington to serve two decades in prison, leaving his wife to raise their two young girls while trying to hold their long-distance marriage together.

His $1.15-per-hour prison wages didn't even cover the bills for the phone calls and marathon bus trips to visit him. Struggling to pay rent and buy food, Ms. Hamilton ended up homeless a couple of times.

"Basically, I was locked up with him," she said. "My mind was locked up. My life was locked up. Our daughters grew up without their father."

The shift to tougher penal policies three decades ago was originally credited with helping people in poor neighborhoods by reducing crime. But now that America's incarceration rate has risen to be the world's highest, many social scientists find the social benefits to be far outweighed by the costs to those communities.

"Prison has become the new poverty trap," said Bruce Western, a Harvard sociologist. "It has become a routine event for poor African-American men and their families, creating an enduring disadvantage at the very bottom of American society."

Among African-Americans who have grown up during the era of mass incarceration, one in four has had a parent locked up at some point during childhood. For black men in their 20s and early 30s without a high school diploma, the incarceration rate is so high —

nearly 40 percent nationwide — that they're more likely to be behind bars than to have a job.

No one denies that some people belong in prison. Mr. Harris, now 47, and his wife, 45, agree that in his early 20s he deserved to be there. But they don't see what good was accomplished by keeping him there for two decades, and neither do most of the researchers who have been analyzing the prison boom.

The number of Americans in state and federal prisons has quintupled since 1980, and a major reason is that prisoners serve longer terms than before. They remain inmates into middle age and old age, well beyond the peak age for crime, which is in the late teenage years — just when Mr. Harris first got into trouble.

'I JUST LOST MY COOL'

After dropping out of high school, Mr. Harris ended up working at a carwash and envying the imports driven by drug dealers. One day in 1983, at the age of 18, while walking with his girlfriend on a sidewalk in Washington where drugs were being sold, he watched a high-level dealer pull up in a Mercedes-Benz and demand money from an underling.

"This dealer was draped down in jewelry and a nice outfit," Mr. Harris recalled in an interview in the Woodridge neighborhood of northeast Washington, where he and his wife now live. "The female with him was draped down, too, gold and everything, dressed real good.

"I'm watching the way he carries himself, and I'm standing there looking like Raggedy Ann. My girl's looking like Raggedy Ann. I said to myself, 'That's what I want to do.' "

Within two years, he was convicted of illegal gun possession, an occupational hazard of his street business selling PCP and cocaine. He went to Lorton, the local prison, in 1985, shortly after he and Ms. Hamilton had their first daughter. He kept up his drug dealing while in prison — "It was just as easy to sell inside as outside" — and returned to the streets for the heyday of the crack market in the late 1980s.

The Washington police never managed to catch him with the cocaine he was importing by the kilo from New York, but they arrested him for assaulting people at a crack den. He says he went into the apartment, in the Shaw neighborhood, to retrieve $4,000 worth of crack stolen by one of his customers, and discovered it was already being smoked by a dozen people in the room.

"I just lost my cool," he said. "I grabbed a lamp and chair lying around there and started smacking people. Nobody was hospitalized, but I broke someone's arm and cut another one in the leg."

An assault like that would have landed Mr. Harris behind bars in many countries, but not for nearly so long. Prisoners serve significantly more time in the United States than in most industrialized countries. Sentences for drug-related offenses and other crimes have gotten stiffer in recent decades, and prosecutors have become more aggressive in seeking longer terms — as Mr. Harris discovered when he saw the multiple charges against him.

For injuring two people, Mr. Harris was convicted on two counts of assault, each carrying a minimum three-year sentence. But he received a much stiffer sentence, of 15 to 45 years, on a charge of armed burglary at the crack den.

"The cops knew I was selling but couldn't prove it, so they made up the burglary charge instead," Mr. Harris contended. He still considers the burglary charge unfair, insisting that he neither broke into the crack den nor took anything, but he also acknowledges that long prison terms were a risk for any American selling drugs: "I knew other dealers who got life without parole."

As it was, at the age of 24 he was facing prison until his mid-40s. He urged his wife to move on with her life and divorce him. Despondent, he began snorting heroin in prison — the first time, he says, that he had ever used hard drugs himself.

"I thought I was going to lose my mind," he said. "I felt so bad leaving my wife alone with our daughters. When they were young, they'd ask on the phone where I was, and I'd tell them I was away at camp."

Carl Harris rejoined his wife, Charlene Hamilton, and their two daughters after 20 years in prison.

His wife went on welfare and turned to relatives to care for their daughters while she visited him at prisons in Tennessee, Texas, Arizona and New Mexico.

"I wanted to work, but I couldn't have a job and go visit him," Ms. Hamilton said. "When he was in New Mexico, it would take me three days to get there on the bus. I'd go out there and stay for a month in a trailer near the prison."

In Washington, she and her daughters moved from relative to relative, not always together. During one homeless spell, Ms. Hamilton slept by herself for a month in her car. She eventually found a federally subsidized apartment of her own, and once the children were in school she took part-time jobs. But the scrimping never stopped. "We had a lot of Oodles of Noodles," she recalled.

Eleven years after her husband went to prison, Ms. Hamilton followed his advice to divorce, but she didn't remarry. Like other women in communities with high rates of incarceration, she faced a shortage of potential mates. Because more than 90 percent of prisoners are men, their absence skews the gender ratio. In some neighborhoods in Washington, there are 6 men for every 10 women.

"With so many men locked up, the ones left think they can do whatever they want," Ms. Hamilton said. "A man will have three mistresses, and they'll each put up with it because there are no other men around."

Epidemiologists have found that when the incarceration rate rises in a county, there tends to be a subsequent increase in the rates of sexually transmitted diseases and teenage pregnancy, possibly because women have less power to require their partners to practice protected sex or remain monogamous.

When researchers try to explain why AIDS is much more prevalent among blacks than whites, they point to the consequences of incarceration, which disrupts steady relationships and can lead to high-risk sexual behavior. When sociologists look for causes of child poverty and juvenile delinquency, they link these problems to the incarceration of parents and the resulting economic and emotional strains on families.

Some families, of course, benefit after an abusive parent or spouse is locked up. But Christopher Wildeman, a Yale sociologist, has found that children are generally more likely to suffer academically and socially after the incarceration of a parent. Boys left fatherless become more physically aggressive. Spouses of prisoners become more prone to depression and other mental and physical problems.

"Education, income, housing, health — incarceration affects everyone and everything in the nation's low-income neighborhoods," said Megan Comfort, a sociologist at the nonprofit research organization RTI International who has analyzed what she calls the "secondary prisonization" of women with partners serving time in San Quentin State Prison.

Before the era of mass incarceration, there was already evidence linking problems in poor neighborhoods to the high number of single-parent households and also to the high rate of mobility: the continual turnover on many blocks as transients moved in and out.

Now those trends have been amplified by the prison boom's "coercive mobility," as it is termed by Todd R. Clear, the dean of the School of Criminal Justice at Rutgers University. In some low-income neighborhoods, he notes, virtually everyone has at least one relative currently or recently behind bars, so families and communities are continually disrupted by people going in and out of prison.

A PERVERSE EFFECT

This social disorder may ultimately have the perverse effect of raising the crime rate in some communities, Dr. Clear and some other scholars say. Robert DeFina and Lance Hannon, both at Villanova University, have found that while crime may initially decline in places that lock up more people, within a few years the rate rebounds and is even higher than before.

New York City's continuing drop in crime in the past two decades may have occurred partly because it reduced its prison population in the 1990s and thereby avoided a subsequent rebound effect.

Raymond V. Liedka, of Oakland University in Michigan, and colleagues have found that the crime-fighting effects of prison disappear once the incarceration rate gets too high. "If the buildup goes beyond a tipping point, then additional incarceration is not going to gain our society any reduction in crime, and may lead to increased crime," Dr. Liedka said.

The benefits of incarceration are especially questionable for men serving long sentences into middle age. The likelihood of committing a crime drops steeply once a man enters his 30s. This was the case with Mr. Harris, who turned his life around shortly after hitting 30.

"I said, 'I wasn't born in no jail, and I'm not going to die here,' " he recalled, describing how he gave up heroin and other drugs, converted to Islam and went to work on his high school equivalency degree.

But he still had 14 more years to spend in prison. During that time, he stayed in touch with his family, talking to his children daily. When he was released in 2009, he reunited with them and Ms. Hamilton.

"I was like a man coming out of a cave after 20 years," Mr. Harris said. "The streets were the same, but everything else had changed. My kids were grown. They had to teach me how to use a cellphone and pay for the bus."

The only job he could find was at a laundry, where he sorted soiled linens for $8.25 an hour, less than half the typical wage for a man his age but not unusual for someone just out of prison. Even though the District of Columbia has made special efforts to find jobs for ex-prisoners and to destigmatize their records — they are officially known as "returning citizens" — many have a hard time finding any kind of work.

This is partly because of employers' well-documented reluctance to hire anyone with a record, partly because of former prisoners' lack of work experience and contacts, and partly because of their difficulties adapting to life after prison.

"You spend long enough in prison being constantly treated like a dog or a parrot, you can get so institutionalized you can't function outside," Mr. Harris said. "That was my biggest challenge, telling myself that I'm not going to forget how to take care of myself or think for myself. I saw that happen to too many guys."

'CRIPPLED BY INCARCERATION'

The Rev. Kelly Wilkins sees men like that every day during her work at the Covenant Baptist Church in Washington, which serves the low-income neighborhoods east of the Anacostia River.

"A lot of the men have been away so long that they're been crippled by incarceration," she said. "They don't know how to survive in the community anymore, and they figure it's too late for someone in their 40s to start life over."

A stint behind bars tends to worsen job prospects that weren't good to begin with. "People who go to prison would have very low wages even without incarceration," said Dr. Western, the Harvard sociologist and author of "Punishment and Inequality in America." "They have very little education, on average, and they live in communities with

With a new outlook on life, Carl Harris returned to his family in 2009. He works as a security guard.

poor job opportunities, and so on. For all this, the balance of the social science evidence shows that prison makes things worse."

Dr. Western and Becky Pettit, a sociologist at the University of Washington, estimate, after controlling for various socioeconomic factors, that incarceration typically reduces annual earnings by 40 percent for the typical male former prisoner.

The precise financial loss is debatable. Other social scientists have come up with lower estimates for lost wages after incarceration, but everyone agrees it's only part of the cost. For starters, it doesn't include wages lost while a man is behind bars.

Nor does it include all the burdens borne by the prisoner's family and community during incarceration — the greatest cost of all, says Donald Braman, an anthropologist at George Washington University Law School who wrote "Doing Time on the Outside" after studying families of prisoners in Washington.

"The social deprivation and draining of capital from these communities may well be the greatest contribution our state makes to income inequality," Dr. Braman said. "There is no social institution I can think of that comes close to matching it."

Drs. DeFina and Hannon, the Villanova sociologists, calculate that if the mass incarceration trend had not occurred in recent decades, the poverty rate would be 20 percent lower today, and that five million fewer people would have fallen below the poverty line.

Ms. Hamilton and Mr. Harris have now risen above that poverty line, and they consider their family luckier than many others. Their two daughters finished high school; one went to college; both are employed. Ms. Hamilton is working as an aide at a hospital. Mr. Harris has a job as a security guard and a different outlook on life.

"I don't worry about buying clothes anymore," he said. He and his wife are scrimping to save enough so they can finally, in their late 40s, buy a home together.

"It's like our life is finally beginning," Ms. Hamilton said. "If he hadn't been away so long, we could own a house by now. We would probably have more kids. I try not to think about all the things we lost."

ACCENTUATING THE POSITIVE

She and her husband prefer to accentuate the positive, even when it comes to the police and prison. They appreciate that some neighborhoods in Washington are much safer now that drug dealers aren't fighting on street corners and in crack dens anymore. They figure the crackdown on open-air drug markets helped both the city and Mr. Harris.

"If I hadn't been locked up, I probably would have ended up getting killed on the streets," Mr. Harris said. His wife agreed.

"Prison was good for him in some ways," Ms. Hamilton said. "He finally grew up there. He's a man now."

But 20 years?

"They overdid it," she said. "It didn't have to take that long at all."

Los Angeles to Reduce Arrest Rate in Schools

BY JENNIFER MEDINA | AUG. 18, 2014

LOS ANGELES — After years of arresting students for on-campus fights and damaging school property, Los Angeles school officials are adopting new policies to reduce the number of students who are disciplined in the juvenile court system.

Under new policies expected to be introduced Tuesday, students who deface school property, participate in an on-campus fights or are caught with tobacco will no longer be given citations by officers from the Los Angeles School Police Department. Instead, they will be dealt with by school officials.

The Los Angeles Unified School District is the second-largest school system in the country, behind New York City, but has the largest school police force, with more than 350 armed officers.

A report last year by the Labor/Community Strategy Center, a civil rights group, found that students at Los Angeles schools were far more likely to receive a criminal citation than students in Chicago, Philadelphia or New York.

Several studies, including one released last year by the federal Education Department's Office of Civil Rights, have found that black and Latino students are far more likely to face harsh disciplinary procedures. A department study released this year found that black students faced more severe discipline as early as preschool: Nearly half of all preschool children suspended were African-American.

Michael Nash, the presiding judge of the Los Angeles Juvenile Courts, who was involved in creating the new policies, said that the juvenile justice system was overtaxed, and that the changes would ensure that the courts were dealing only with youngsters who "really pose the greatest risk to the community."

The Los Angeles Unified School District is the second-largest school system in the country, behind New York City, but has the largest school police force, with more than 350 armed officers.

"There are enough studies that show bringing them into the justice system is really more of a slippery slope that leads to negative outcomes and poor futures," Judge Nash said. "The people who are in these schools need to deal with these issues, not use the courts as an outlet. We have to change our attitude and realize that the punitive approach clearly hasn't worked."

Judge Nash cited examples of students who were sent to court for using profanity while arguing with a teacher.

"What is the court going to do? The kid is going to lose a day of school, and the family is going to get a fine they aren't going to be able to afford," he said. "What's the point of that?"

Both Attorney General Eric H. Holder Jr. and Education Secretary Arne Duncan have decried the negative impact of "zero tolerance" policies. National studies have also shown that students are more likely to drop out if they are arrested, and many advocates have long criticized harsh discipline as part of what they call the "school to prison pipeline."

School systems in Northern California and Georgia have also made similar changes in recent years.

"We want schools to be a place where kids are pre-med or pre-jobs, not pre-prison," said Manuel Criollo, the director of organizing at the Labor/Community Strategy Center, which has pushed for the changes in the district for years. "Students really have been profiled inside the school setting, instead of getting the help they need from school counselors."

Students 14 years old and under received more than 45 percent of the district's 1,360 citations in 2013, according to the Strategy Center. African-American students, who account for about 10 percent of the total population, received 39 percent of "disturbing the peace" citations, typically given for fights.

A citation is referred to the county Probation Department, which can then prevent teenagers from receiving a driver's license. An arrest usually leads to a mandatory appearance in Juvenile Court for the student and his or her parents, and often a fine. Cases of arrested students are passed to the district attorney, who decides whether or not to pursue charges.

"We're talking about schoolyard fights that a couple of decades ago nobody would have ever thought would lead to arrest," said Ruth Cusick, an education rights lawyer for Public Counsel, a nonprofit group that helped draft the new policies. "The criminalizing of this behavior only goes on in low-income communities."

In 2012, Los Angeles school officials stopped citing students who arrived late for class. That has reduced the number of citations for absent students by more than 90 percent, while attendance rates have largely stayed steady or improved, Judge Nash said.

Jails Have Become Warehouses for the Poor, Ill and Addicted, a Report Says

BY TIMOTHY WILLIAMS | FEB. 11, 2015

JAILS ACROSS THE COUNTRY have become vast warehouses made up primarily of people too poor to post bail or too ill with mental health or drug problems to adequately care for themselves, according to a report issued Wednesday.

The study, "Incarceration's Front Door: The Misuse of Jails in America," found that the majority of those incarcerated in local and county jails are there for minor violations, including driving with suspended licenses, shoplifting or evading subway fares, and have been jailed for longer periods of time over the past 30 years because they are unable to pay court-imposed costs.

The report, by the Vera Institute of Justice, comes at a time of increased attention to mass incarceration policies that have swelled prison and jail populations around the country. This week in Missouri, where the fatal shooting of an unarmed black man by a white police officer stirred months of racial tension last year in the town of Ferguson, 15 people sued that city and another suburb, Jennings, alleging that the cities created an unconstitutional modern-day debtors' prison, putting impoverished people behind bars in overcrowded, unlawful and unsanitary conditions.

While most reform efforts, including early releases and the elimination of some minimum mandatory sentences, have been focused on state and federal prisons, the report found that the disparate rules that apply to jails are also in need of reform.

"It's an important moment to take a look at our use of jails," said Nancy Fishman, the project director of the Vera Institute's Center on Sentencing and Corrections and an author of the report. "It's a huge burden on taxpayers, on our communities, and we need to decide if this is how we want to spend our resources."

The number of people housed in jails on any given day in the country has increased from 224,000 in 1983 to 731,000 in 2013 — nearly equal to the population of Charlotte, N.C. — even as violent crime nationally has fallen by nearly 50 percent and property crime has dropped by more than 40 percent from its peak.

Inmates have subsequently been spending more time in jail awaiting trial, in part because of the growing reluctance of judges to free suspects on their own recognizance pending trial dates, which had once been common for minor offenses.

As a result, many of those accused of misdemeanors — who are often poor — are unable to pay bail as low as $500.

Timed with the release of the Vera Institute report, the MacArthur Foundation announced Wednesday that it would invest $75 million over five years in 20 jurisdictions that are seeking alternatives to sending large numbers of people to jail. The jurisdictions, which could be cities, counties or other entities that run local jails, will be announced this spring.

Nationwide, the annual number of jail admissions is 19 times higher than the number of those sent to prison, and has nearly doubled since 1983, from about 6 million to 11.7 million. A significant number are repeat offenders, the report said.

In Chicago, for instance, 21 percent of the people sent to local jails from 2007 to 2011 accounted for 50 percent of all jail admissions.

In New York City, the figures were even starker: From 2009 to 2013, about 400 people were sent to jail on at least 18 occasions each, which accounted for more than 10,000 jail admissions and 300,000 days in jail.

The study found that the share of people in jail accused or convicted of crimes related to illegal drugs increased from 9 percent in 1983 to about 25 percent in 2013, and that they were disproportionately African-Americans.

And the study said that while 68 percent of jail inmates had a history of abusing drugs, alcohol or both, jail-based drug treatment programs had been underfunded.

Justin Volpe, 31, a peer recovery specialist in Miami for the Dade County courts, said he spent 45 days in jail in 2007 after being arrested on a petty theft charge. Mr. Volpe, who was homeless, addicted to drugs and suffering from an untreated mental illness at the time of his arrest, said drug treatment and a court-mandated diversion program that included counseling and medication had probably saved his life.

"It was the extra push I needed," he said.

But Mr. Volpe said there were too few drug and alcohol treatment programs available to those in jail, where there is a close correlation between drug addiction and mental illness.

The Vera Institute report, for instance, found that more than four of five inmates with a mental illness were not treated in jail and that 34 percent of those with mental illness in jail had been using drugs at the time of their arrest, compared with 20 percent of the rest of the jail population.

Still, seeking mental health services sometimes meant longer stints in jail, the report said. In Los Angeles, those seeking help spent more than twice as much time in custody than did others — 43 days, compared with 18 days.

Why American Prisons Owe Their Cruelty to Slavery

BY BRYAN STEVENSON | AUG. 14, 2019

Slavery gave America a fear of black people and a taste for punishment. Both still define our criminal justice system.

SEVERAL YEARS AGO, my law office was fighting for the release of a black man who had been condemned, at the age of 16, to die in prison. Matthew was one of 62 Louisiana children sentenced to life imprisonment without parole for nonhomicide offenses. But a case I'd argued at the Supreme Court was part of a 2010 ruling that banned such sentences for juveniles, making our clients eligible for release.

Some had been in prison for nearly 50 years. Almost all had been sent to Angola, a penitentiary considered one of America's most violent and abusive. Angola is immense, larger than Manhattan, covering land once occupied by slave plantations. Our clients there worked in fields under the supervision of horse-riding, shotgun-toting guards who forced them to pick crops, including cotton. Their disciplinary records show that if they refused to pick cotton — or failed to pick it fast enough — they could be punished with time in "the hole," where food was restricted and inmates were sometimes tear-gassed. Still, some black prisoners, including Matthew, considered the despair of the hole preferable to the unbearable degradation of being forced to pick cotton on a plantation at the end of the 20th century. I was fearful that such clients would be denied parole based on their disciplinary records. Some were.

The United States has the highest rate of incarceration of any nation on Earth: We represent 4 percent of the planet's population but 22 percent of its imprisoned. In the early 1970s, our prisons held fewer than 300,000 people; since then, that number has grown to more than 2.2 million, with 4.5 million more on probation or parole. Because of mandatory sentencing and "three-strikes" laws, I've found myself representing clients sentenced to life without parole for stealing a bicycle or for simple possession of marijuana. And central to understanding this practice of mass incarceration and excessive punishment is the legacy of slavery.

IT TOOK ONLY a few decades after the arrival of enslaved Africans in Virginia before white settlers demanded a new world defined by racial caste. The 1664 General Assembly of Maryland decreed that all Negroes within the province "shall serve *durante vita*," hard labor for life. This enslavement would be sustained by the threat of brutal punishment. By 1729, Maryland law authorized punishments of enslaved people including "to have the right hand cut off … the head severed from the body, the body divided into four quarters, and head and quarters set up in the most public places of the county."

Soon American slavery matured into a perverse regime that denied the humanity of black people while still criminalizing their actions. As the Supreme Court of Alabama explained in 1861, enslaved black people were "capable of committing crimes," and in that capacity were "regarded as persons" — but in most every other sense they were "incapable of performing civil acts" and considered "things, not persons."

The 13th Amendment is credited with ending slavery, but it stopped short of that: It made an exception for those convicted of crimes. After emancipation, black people, once seen as less than fully human "slaves," were seen as less than fully human "criminals." The provisional governor of South Carolina declared in 1865 that they had to be "restrained from theft, idleness, vagrancy and crime." Laws governing slavery were replaced with Black Codes governing free black people — making the criminal-justice system central to new strategies of racial control.

These strategies intensified whenever black people asserted their independence or achieved any measure of success. During Reconstruction, the emergence of black elected officials and entrepreneurs was countered by convict leasing, a scheme in which white policymakers invented offenses used to target black people: vagrancy, loitering, being a group of black people out after dark, seeking employment without a note from a former enslaver. The imprisoned were then "leased" to businesses and farms, where they labored under brutal conditions. An 1887 report in Mississippi found that six months after 204 prisoners were leased to a white man named McDonald, dozens were dead or dying, the prison hospital filled with men whose bodies bore "marks of the most inhuman and brutal treatment … so poor and emaciated that their bones almost come through the skin."

Anything that challenged the racial hierarchy could be seen as a crime, punished either by the law or by the lynchings that stretched from Mississippi to Minnesota. In 1916, Anthony Crawford was lynched in South Carolina for being successful enough to refuse a low price for his cotton. In 1933, Elizabeth Lawrence was lynched near Birmingham for daring to chastise white children who were throwing rocks at her.

It's not just that this history fostered a view of black people as presumptively criminal. It also cultivated a tolerance for employing any level of brutality in response. In 1904, in Mississippi, a black man was accused of shooting a white landowner who had attacked him. A white mob captured him and the woman with him, cut off their ears and fingers, drilled corkscrews into their flesh and then burned them alive — while hundreds of white spectators enjoyed deviled eggs and lemonade. The landowner's brother, Woods Eastland, presided over the violence; he was later elected district attorney of Scott County, Miss., a position that allowed his son James Eastland, an avowed white supremacist, to serve six terms as a United States senator, becoming president pro tempore from 1972 to 1978.

This appetite for harsh punishment has echoed across the decades. Late in the 20th century, amid protests over civil rights and inequality, a new politics of fear and anger would emerge. Nixon's war on drugs, mandatory minimum sentences, three-strikes laws, children tried as adults, "broken windows" policing — these policies were not as expressly racialized as the Black Codes, but their implementation has been essentially the same. It is black and brown people who are disproportionately targeted, stopped, suspected, incarcerated and shot by the police.

HUNDREDS OF YEARS after the arrival of enslaved Africans, a presumption of danger and criminality still follows black people everywhere. New language has emerged for the noncrimes that have replaced the Black Codes: driving while black, sleeping while black, sitting in a coffee shop while black. All reflect incidents in which African-Americans were mistreated, assaulted or arrested for conduct that would be ignored if they were white. In schools, black kids are suspended and expelled at rates that vastly exceed the punishment of white children for the same behavior.

Inside courtrooms, the problem gets worse. Racial disparities in sentencing are found in almost every crime category. Children as young as 13, almost all black, are sentenced to life imprisonment for nonhomicide offenses. Black defendants are 22 times more likely to receive the death penalty for crimes whose victims are white, rather than black — a type of bias the Supreme Court has declared "inevitable."

The smog created by our history of racial injustice is suffocating and toxic. We are too practiced in ignoring the victimization of any black people tagged as criminal; like Woods Eastland's crowd, too many Americans are willing spectators to horrifying acts, as long as we're assured they're in the interest of maintaining order.

This cannot be the end of the story. In 2018, the Equal Justice Initiative, a nonprofit I direct, opened a museum in Montgomery, Ala., dedicated to the legacy of slavery and a memorial honoring thousands of black lynching victims. We must acknowledge the 400 years of injustice that haunt us. I'm encouraged: Half a million people have visited. But I'm also worried, because we are at one of those critical moments in American history when we will either double down on romanticizing our past or accept that there is something better waiting for us.

I recently went to New Orleans to celebrate the release of several of our Angola clients, including Matthew — men who survived the fields and the hole. I realized how important it is to stay hopeful: Hopelessness is the enemy of justice. There were moments of joy that night. But there was also heaviness; we all seemed keenly aware that we were not truly free from the burden of living in a nation that continues to deny and doubt this legacy, and how much work remains to be done.

BRYAN STEVENSON is the executive director of the Equal Justice Initiative and the author of "Just Mercy: A Story of Justice and Redemption."

CHAPTER 2

Policing Under Scrutiny

Some of the most heated debates around our criminal justice system concern policing. Following "tough on crime" legislation that expanded our prison system, many police departments have adopted policies favoring increased stops, arrests and uses of deadly force — often with high racial disparities. This trend has been strengthened by federal grants of military surplus to police departments. As the Ferguson unrest sparked calls for police reform, many police chiefs answered with attempts to change the daily culture of their local departments, to mixed results.

Beyond Stop-and-Frisk

OPINION | JAMES FORMAN JR. AND TREVOR STUTZ | APRIL 19, 2012

NEW HAVEN — In the face of growing anger over the New York Police Department's stop-and-frisk policy, the commissioner, Raymond W. Kelly, has faulted his critics for failing to offer an alternative for fighting crime in minority neighborhoods. "What I haven't heard is any solution to the violence problems in these communities," he told the City Council last month.

Mr. Kelly is correct that high levels of violence are intolerable and that those who would challenge stop-and-frisk — in which police officers use thin pretexts for streetside searches — must present credible alternatives. At the Yale Law School Innovations in Policing Clinic, we have been visiting police departments around the country in search of such strategies. One increasingly popular approach, "focused deterrence," is among the most promising.

Developed by the criminologist David M. Kennedy, focused deterrence is in many ways the opposite of stopping and frisking large sections of the population. Beginning with the recognition that a small cohort of young men are responsible for most of the violent crime in minority neighborhoods, it targets the worst culprits for intensive investigation and criminal prosecution.

Focused deterrence also builds up community trust in the police, who are now going after the real bad guys instead of harassing innocent bystanders in an effort to score easy arrests.

This strategy was responsible for the dramatic decline in Boston's homicide rate during the 1990s. In 2004, Mr. Kennedy and his colleagues successfully adapted it to combat violent open-air drug markets in the West End neighborhood of High Point, N.C.

Rather than sweep through and stop large numbers of young black men, the police built strong relationships with residents, promising greater responsiveness if they took back the reins of their community and told their sons, nephews and grandsons that the violence and the overt dealing must end. Meanwhile, the police identified the 17 men driving the drug market and built solid cases against each. In one fell swoop, they arrested three with violent records.

The other 14 men were then summoned to a community meeting. Neighborhood residents demanded that they put an end to the violence. Law enforcement officials made credible threats of prosecution, but also told the men they had one last chance to turn their lives around. Meanwhile, social service providers offered them job training, drug treatment and mentoring.

Most of the men listened. The city's most significant drug market vanished overnight, and it has not come back. Violent crime has fallen by half.

Why did the strategy succeed? The Rev. Sherman Mason, a local minister, told us that a key factor was the decision to involve neighborhood residents in the process. As a result, the police gained legitimacy, and their relationship with the community was transformed.

While focused deterrence is among the most thoroughly researched efforts to reduce crime while building community trust, it is not the only one.

In Seattle longtime adversaries, including the police department and the public defender's office, are collaborating on a program to authorize police officers to divert drug offenders to treatment.

In Illinois and in Washington State, efforts are under way to train officers in "procedural justice," in other words, how to operate in a more transparently fair way, as people are more likely to comply with the law if the police treat them with dignity and respect.

New York has a moral imperative to address violence. But stop-and-frisk practices are harming the community in order to protect it, and the costs of those practices can no longer be justified by the claim that nothing else will work. There are other ways.

JAMES FORMAN JR. is a clinical professor at Yale Law school and supervises its Innovations in Policing Clinic, where **TREVOR STUTZ**, a third-year law student, is a member.

Get the Military Off of Main Street

OPINION | BY ELIZABETH R. BEAVERS AND MICHAEL SHANK | AUG. 14, 2014

WASHINGTON — Ferguson, Mo., has become a virtual war zone. In the wake of the shooting of an unarmed black teenager, Michael Brown, outsize armored vehicles have lined streets and tear gas has filled the air. Officers dressed in camouflage uniforms from Ferguson's 53-person police force have pointed M-16s at the very citizens they are sworn to protect and serve.

The police response has shocked America. The escalating tension in this town of 21,200 people between a largely white police department and a majority African-American community is a central part of the crisis, but the militarization of the police is a dimension of the story that has national implications.

Ferguson's police force got equipped this way thanks to the Pentagon, and it's happening all over the country. The Department of Defense provides military-grade weapons and equipment to local law enforcement agencies through the 1033 program, enacted by Congress in 1997 to expand the practice of dispensing extra military gear. Due to the defense industry's bloated contracts, there is a huge surplus. To date, the Pentagon has donated military equipment worth more than $4 billion to local law enforcement agencies. And the giving goes on, to police forces in all 50 states in the union.

Ferguson's police department is just one recipient; small towns all over America are now the proud owners of "MRAP" armored vehicles. The largess has gotten so out of hand that a congressman, Hank C. Johnson, is introducing a bill to block the 1033 handouts.

Whereas the Department of Defense hands over weapons directly, the Department of Homeland Security provides funding for arms. It has distributed more than $34 billion through "terrorism grants," enabling local police departments to acquire such absurd items as a surveillance drone and an Army tank.

For a police department like Ferguson's, the path to becoming a paramilitary force is a short one. After loading up with free military gear, it is no surprise that law enforcement agents want to use it. In fact, the 1033 program's regulations require that the police use what they receive within one year.

In the absence of extreme violence or actual terrorist threat, what happens — as the American Civil Liberties Union has documented — is that the equipment and weapons are used by SWAT teams in routine situations, such as low-level drug raids or the execution of search warrants. As Ferguson shows, this militarizing of routine police work exacerbates tensions and increases the likelihood of disorder. This, in turn, appears to justify a militarized police response, and so the cycle continues.

The federal government can stop this increased militarization at its source. The Pentagon must end its transfer of military-grade weapons through the 1033 program. And the Department of Homeland Security should stop handing out the terrorism grants. The ease with which police departments can avail themselves of Homeland Security funding for enormous caches of weapons and ammunition in the name of counterterrorism is deeply disconcerting.

Veteran police chiefs who have served on the front lines of America's biggest police forces are voicing their concern. Norman H. Stamper, the former police chief of Seattle, has written with regret about the military-style tactics employed during the protests against the 1999 World Trade Organization conference in Seattle; he now advocates "an authentic partnership in policing the city," involving rank-and-file officers, civilian employees and community representatives.

Militarizing our police officers does not have to be the first response to violence. Alternatives are available. Attorney General Eric H. Holder Jr.'s statement Thursday highlighting resources like the Department of Justice's Community Oriented Policing Services office is welcome. This is where the government should be investing — instead of grants for guns.

Police militarization is a growing national threat. If the federal government doesn't act to stop it, the future of law enforcement everywhere will look a lot like Ferguson.

ELIZABETH R. BEAVERS is the legislative associate for militarism and civil liberties, and **MICHAEL SHANK** is the associate director for legislative affairs, at the Friends Committee on National Legislation.

Bratton Says New York
Police Officers Must Fight Bias

BY J. DAVID GOODMAN | FEB. 24, 2015

THE NEW YORK CITY police commissioner, William J. Bratton, on Tuesday delivered a broad commentary on the country's troubled history of race relations and the role of the police in fostering old divisions that still sow distrust in minority communities.

In a 26-minute address that touched on slavery, Peter Stuyvesant and the fatal police shooting of a black teenager in 1964, Mr. Bratton told the story of racial tension through the prism of the police and the "vile" legacy of racism that once sat on a foundation of law and order. "Many of the worst parts of black history would have been impossible without police," he said.

Mr. Bratton, during his address in a crowded church basement in Jamaica, Queens, also addressed the kinds of latent racial biases that may still affect officers and that formed the centerpiece of a striking speech this month by the director of the Federal Bureau of Investigation, James B. Comey.

When officers see "the same young men in the same neighborhoods committing almost all of this city's violence," Mr. Bratton said, it "carries a risk of turning into bias."

He added: "We need to fight against that."

The two speeches, by two of the most prominent figures in policing, highlighted a national effort on the part of law enforcement leaders to turn a corner after months of tension and protest that flared last year over the deaths of two unarmed black men in Ferguson, Mo., and on Staten Island.

Mr. Comey, in his address, cited the song "Everyone's a Little Bit Racist" from the Broadway musical "Avenue Q" and acknowledged that police officers were not immune to bias. He said officers, regardless of their race, viewed white and black men differently.

Commissioner William J. Bratton gave an address on the police and racial tension at a church in Jamaica, Queens, on Tuesday.

Mr. Bratton, for his part, said on Tuesday that while the country and the city were founded on systems of slavery and racism, those unjust systems, which included the police, had since given way to problematic individuals.

"I do not deny that it exists," Mr. Bratton said, speaking of cruelty and injustice by officers. "But it is not systemic in the sense that we do not condone it."

"It is a matter of the actions of the few," he added, "and the few that we need to seek to find and get rid of. And the few that we need to keep out of the ranks of the N.Y.P.D."

At times, Mr. Bratton appeared to build on Mr. Comey's discussion of "hard truths," saying the New York Police Department needed to face its own hard truth: that in minority neighborhoods where crime is high, "we have a problem with citizen satisfaction."

"We're often abrupt, sometimes rude, and that's unacceptable," he said. "But our critics need to face the hard truth that they misrepresent us sometimes."

Mr. Bratton reiterated the need, also expressed in his eulogy for Rafael Ramos, one of two officers killed together in December, for the police and protesters to "see each other."

The speech on Tuesday, part of a Black History Month event, received a warm reception from the mostly black audience, including former Gov. David A. Paterson, in the Greater Allen A.M.E. Church of New York. At the end, many stood to applaud.

Some advocates who have called for a wholesale reform of Mr. Bratton's "broken windows" policing strategy, in which officers focus on minor offenses to prevent major crimes, embraced the long view offered by Mr. Bratton. But they challenged the notion that the problems were no longer systemic.

"Commissioner Bratton is in the position of authority now to address current problems of discriminatory policing in New York City," Priscilla Gonzalez, a spokeswoman for Communities United for Police Reform, said. "Unless he takes action, he, too, will be judged poorly by history."

Chicago Police Dept. Plagued by Systemic Racism, Task Force Finds

BY MONICA DAVEY AND MITCH SMITH | APRIL 13, 2016

CHICAGO — Racism has contributed to a long pattern of institutional failures by the Chicago Police Department in which officers have mistreated people, operated without sufficient oversight, and lost the trust of residents, a task force appointed by Mayor Rahm Emanuel has found.

The report, issued on Wednesday, was blistering, blunt and backed up by devastating statistics. Coincidentally, it was released as city leaders were installing a new, permanent superintendent for the Chicago Police Department.

"C.P.D.'s own data gives validity to the widely held belief the police have no regard for the sanctity of life when it comes to people of color," the task force wrote. "Stopped without justification, verbally and physically abused, and in some instances arrested, and then detained without counsel — that is what we heard about over and over again."

The report reinforces complaints made for decades by African-American residents who have said they were unfairly singled out by officers without justification on a regular basis, then ignored when they raised complaints.

It comes at a pivotal moment for the nation's second-largest municipal police force, which is being criticized by residents and is under scrutiny from the Justice Department. And, coming from Mr. Emanuel's own appointees, the findings intensify pressure on him and other Chicago leaders to make substantive, swift changes.

The report makes more than 100 specific recommendations for change, and task force members called on the mayor and the City Council to take action. After formally receiving the report, Mr. Emanuel had no immediate public reaction.

The task force amassed data that shows the extent to which African-Americans appear to have been disproportionately focused on by the police. In a city where whites, blacks and Hispanics each make up about one-third of the population, 74 percent of the 404 people shot by the Chicago police between 2008 and 2015 were black, the report said. Black people were the subjects in 72 percent of the thousands of investigative street stops that did not lead to arrests during the summer of 2014.

Three out of every four people on whom Chicago police officers tried to use Taser guns between 2012 and 2015 were black. And black drivers made up 46 percent of police traffic stops in 2013.

"The community's lack of trust in C.P.D. is justified," according to the report, a draft summary of which was first reported in The Chicago Tribune on Tuesday afternoon. "There is substantial evidence that people of color — particularly African-Americans — have had disproportionately negative experiences with the police over an extended period of time."

The stinging findings come at a particularly volatile time here, as violent crimes have increased this year and as police morale is reported to have sunk. Murders are up 62 percent this year compared with a year ago, Chicago police statistics show, and shootings have increased by 78 percent.

Public pressure has remained intense. Just this week, after an officer fatally shot a black 16-year-old who the police said was armed, protesters took to the streets.

The task force was given its assignment late last year, after the release of a graphic dashcam video showing a white Chicago police officer, Jason Van Dyke, fatally shooting a black teenager, Laquan McDonald, along a Chicago street. Widespread protests followed, and Mr. Emanuel fired the city's police superintendent. He was officially replaced on Wednesday by the mayor's choice, Eddie Johnson, a longtime Chicago officer who is black, grew up in a public housing project, and lives on the city's South Side.

In picking Mr. Johnson, Mr. Emanuel sidestepped a city requirement that he select a superintendent from finalists chosen by a police board, and the City Council unanimously approved the choice on Wednesday.

Eddie Johnson, left, shook hands on Wednesday with Mayor Rahm Emanuel of Chicago after being sworn in as the new police superintendent.

The task force members were racially diverse, with professional backgrounds in social work, law and government. Lori Lightfoot, the president of the Chicago Police Board, an oversight group, was chairwoman, and the panel was advised by Deval Patrick, the former Massachusetts governor, who spent part of his childhood in Chicago.

"What we heard from people all across the city is they felt like they didn't even have a claim to the geography in front of their house, on their street, or in their neighborhoods," Ms. Lightfoot said, as she presented the report at a downtown library. She acknowledged high rates of violence in some of those communities, but said that did not excuse abuses of power by the police, and that officers must be trained to fight crime while also respecting residents' rights.

The panel described the city's delays in releasing the Laquan McDonald video and officials' false descriptions of what had happened in the days immediately after that shooting as a "tipping point" for long-simmering anger. But "the linkage between racism and C.P.D." had not bubbled up only after the McDonald video was made public, it said. Rather, Mr. McDonald's death gave voice to years of unfair treatment, distrust within minority communities, and to "the deaths of numerous men and women of color whose lives came to an end solely because of an encounter with C.P.D.," the report said.

"The task force heard over and over again from a range of voices, particularly from African-Americans, that some C.P.D. officers are racist, have no respect for the lives and experiences of people of color and approach every encounter with people of color as if the person, regardless of age, gender or circumstance, is a criminal," the report said, adding later, "These encounters leave an indelible mark."

"Even if there was no arrest," it said, "there is a lasting, negative effect."

The report also condemned aspects of the city's contracts with police unions, calling for changes to clauses that they said "make it easy for officers to lie in official reports," ban anonymous citizen complaints and prevent the department from rewarding officers who turn in rule-breaking colleagues. The contracts, the task force concluded, "have essentially turned the code of silence into official policy." The president of the union that represents rank-and-file officers did not immediately respond to interview requests.

The report calls for dissolving the Independent Police Review Authority, which is charged with overseeing the most serious claims of police misconduct. The task force concluded that the authority has failed to investigate a large segment of its cases, rarely carries out meaningful discipline, and is perceived as favoring the police. It recommended that it be replaced with a "fully transparent and accountable civilian police investigative agency."

The report also calls for an expansion of the city's body cam program; a unit assigned to handle issues around mental health crises; and a new deputy chief at the department in charge of diversity and inclusion. It also recommended putting in place a citywide reconciliation process in which the superintendent would publicly acknowledge the department's history of racial disparity and discrimination and make a public commitment to change.

The recommendations and the report drew praise for their candor, but some here remained doubtful about whether it would really bring widespread change.

"The strong diagnoses must be followed by action — by the mayor, the City Council and the Police Department," said Karen Sheley, police practices director for the American Civil Liberties Union of Illinois. "Corrective measures — those outlined by the task force and others — must be fashioned in a way that they cannot be reversed."

Charlene A. Carruthers, national director of Black Youth Project 100, a Chicago-based activist organization, said that she had not yet reviewed the report, but that she considered the task force "yet another example of the mayor's office and those in power in the city of Chicago making decisions on behalf of the community."

Ms. Carruthers said increased civilian oversight and changes to police union contracts — two task force recommendations — were urgently needed. But, she added, "I do not have confidence that the task force or the mayor's office will take bold enough steps."

On Wednesday, before the report was released, Mr. Emanuel said that his "general attitude" was to be "open to look at everything they say." He met with members of his task force late in the day, but did not comment on the report afterward.

Earlier in the day, Mr. Emanuel had said he wanted to work through the issues.

"I don't really think you need a task force to know that we have racism in America, we have racism in Illinois, or that there's racism that exists in the city of Chicago and obviously could be in our department," he said.

He added: "The question is: What are we going to do to confront it and make the changes in not only personnel but in policies to reflect, I think, the values that make up the diversity of our city?"

The Lives of Ferguson Activists, Five Years Later

BY TIMOTHY WILLIAMS AND JOHN ELIGON | AUG. 9, 2019

The energy of the street protests has faded, but it carries on in national conversations about race, and in the lives of the people who were there.

IT WASN'T UNTIL the QuikTrip gas station was burned and looted on Aug. 10, 2014, that the protests began to take hold in the public consciousness. The day before, the body of Michael Brown, a young black man fatally shot by a white police officer, was left lying for hours on a street in Ferguson, Mo., while a disparate group of people gathered in anger.

What happened in Ferguson is often described as a catalyst — the beginning of a social justice movement that would sweep the nation. Five years later, the energy of the street protests has faded, but it carries on in national conversations about racial inequality, white privilege, reparations and police misconduct. It also lives on in the people who were there.

These seven women and men represent the broad array of activists who emerged from the demonstrations in Ferguson. Their stories show the steep price that many paid as well as the opportunities they found to effect change.

'THEY ALSO HAVE TO FORGIVE THEMSELVES.'

Michael Brown Sr. avoids "ground zero," the patch of asphalt on Canfield Drive where he arrived to find his son, whose body had been left under a blazing sun for hours. Over time, and with great difficulty, Mr. Brown, who jokes that his stern demeanor sometimes frightens strangers, has transformed himself from grieving, angry parent to full-time peace activist.

The ability to forgive, he said, has been essential. "I turned my pain into purpose, and turned my anger into a positive," he said. "And I'm not going to stop until I stop ticking." After Michael Brown Jr. was

Michael Brown Sr. in New York in 2018.

killed, Mr. Brown and Lesley McSpadden, Michael's mother and Mr. Brown's ex-wife, shared a $1.5 million wrongful death settlement. Each parent has set up a charitable foundation. Mr. Brown now travels the nation trying to keep other families from experiencing the grief that only the parents of dead children know.

He has marched with the relatives of other African-Americans killed by the police — Tamir Rice, Eric Garner and Akai Gurley, among them — and has lobbied Congress to fund body cameras for police departments. He speaks to whomever is willing to listen: elected officials, parents, children. "I go to elementary schools and I make sure I go talk to the worst and the baddest kids," he said.

Mr. Brown, 41, has spent the past month speaking about forgiveness to groups of prison inmates in South Carolina. "It's something the guys really embrace because there is someone they want to forgive them," he said. "They also have to forgive themselves. Their lives have stopped, but the world has kept on moving along."

'IT WASN'T SOMETHING HE TALKED ABOUT.'

Edward Crawford Jr. is the subject of one of the most memorable photographs taken during the Ferguson protests. In it, he wears an American flag T-shirt while hurling a blazing can of tear gas. The photo was reproduced on T-shirts and mugs. It helped The St. Louis Post-Dispatch win a Pulitzer Prize for photography. It even became a tattoo.

The image led to a life of recognition for Mr. Crawford. Strangers approached him for his autograph. People sought him out for selfies. But friends say Mr. Crawford was never able to distance himself from the fame. "People would run up and want to take pictures with him, and he would be polite," said Tony Rice, an activist who met Mr. Crawford during the protests. "But I don't think I ever heard him mention it. It wasn't something he talked about."

And then, more than one year after the photo was taken, St. Louis County filed Ferguson-related charges against Mr. Crawford for interfering with a police officer and assault. The case was pending in May 2017 when Mr. Crawford was found dead with a gunshot wound to the head in the back seat of a car. He was 27.

Mr. Crawford never made any money from the photo. "We were working through 'how to deal with being famous,'" Jerryl T. Christmas, his lawyer, said. On the day Mr. Crawford died, he had missed a meeting with Mr. Christmas about a plea deal that would have allowed him to avoid jail time.

Though Mr. Crawford's death has been ruled a suicide, questions have persisted among those who knew him. He is one of at least six activists with connections to Ferguson who have died violently, some from apparent suicides.

IT WAS A 'CRASH COURSE IN LIFE.'

Alisha Sonnier was an 18-year-old black woman preparing for college in August 2014, and so she saw the tragedy of Michael Brown's death in very personal terms. They were the same age and preparing for the next chapters in their lives. Only he would never get to see it.

Alisha Sonnier in St. Louis in 2019.

She became a part of the nightly protests and, along with Jonathan Pulphus, a friend and classmate at St. Louis University, helped to start Tribe X, an activist group. They staged the first major "die-in" in St. Louis, during which protesters lay in the streets of a popular entertainment district.

Ms. Sonnier, now 23, said Ferguson was a "crash course in life" that helped to push her into activism. She worked on the political campaigns of local progressive candidates. She helped to introduce Bernie Sanders at an area rally during the 2016 presidential race. She has traveled to college campuses around the country to discuss student activism.

She entered college wanting to become a biomedical engineer who made a lot of money. After Ferguson, she realized she needed to be in a job that would allow her to interact with people, she said. She is now expected to graduate in December with degrees in psychology and African-American studies.

In 2017, Ms. Sonnier transferred to the University of Missouri-St. Louis to distance herself from some of the emotional baggage of her earlier campus activism. She battled mental health issues, an experience that inspired her to try to organize a mental health fair in the city. "The most important thing to me in a career is not money," she said. "I think about how do I want my career to impact my community and to impact the people in it."

'WHEN LESS PEOPLE ARE KILLED, I'LL BE HAPPY AND PROUD.'

About a week after Michael Brown was killed, DeRay Mckesson watched the chaotic protests unfold from his home in Minneapolis, where he worked in human resources for the city's school district. "I remember sitting on the couch and being like, 'I can't give these internal speeches about my commitment to young people and not at least go for a weekend,'" Mr. Mckesson said.

He headed to Ferguson and became one of the most recognizable — and divisive — figures to emerge from the protests.

Mr. Mckesson is praised for helping to shape the national conversation around race and policing, but he is also derided as a "celebrity activist" more interested in publicity than advancing the cause of social justice. Since the initial response to Ferguson, Mr. Mckesson, 34, has seen his Twitter following grow from 800 to a million. He has written a memoir and spent time among Hollywood's black elite.

"I think people use the phrase 'celebrity activist' as a way to distance me from the work, to say, 'He is more focused on his platform than work,'" Mr. Mckesson said. "It's never been true." Mr. Mckesson said he leveraged the influence of celebrities to effect change. With other Ferguson activists he created Campaign Zero, an initiative to end police violence. The group has met with numerous presidential candidates.

Now Mr. Mckesson splits time between his native Baltimore, where he ran unsuccessfully for mayor in 2016, and New York. Making a living through speaking, his book and a podcast, he continues to call for changes in policing and says he remains frustrated by the persistence of officer-involved shootings. "I was part of helping to change the conversation around the country and the world," he said. "When less people are killed, I'll be happy and proud."

'I'LL ALWAYS BE A FERGUSON PROTESTER.'

In August 2014, Johnetta Elzie was attempting to pull her life back together. That year her mother had died of complications from lupus, and a friend in the St. Louis area had been killed by the police. She struggled through the anguish and was preparing for cosmetology school. Then came the death of Michael Brown. Ms. Elzie went to the scene that night and returned day after day, even as police officers showed up in riot gear and armored vehicles.

Ms. Elzie became a fixture on the streets and an authority of the protests on Twitter. In 2016, she appeared on the cover of Essence. That was the peak before a downward spiral. Ms. Elzie, 30, said she was sexually assaulted that year. The trauma was especially difficult

DEMETRIUS FREEMAN FOR THE NEW YORK TIMES

Johnetta Elzie in St. Louis in 2019.

given that she had just spent two years protesting police violence. "It was like, 'Do you call the police?' " she said. "And if I call the police, are they going to kill him, or kill me, or kill us both?"

She deleted her Twitter and Facebook accounts in the summer of 2017 and moved to San Francisco. She went from a constant presence online to disappearing from public view.

She has since moved back to St. Louis and returned to social media, saying she wanted to tell her story as an example of the toll that non-stop activism can have on a person's mental health. "I think I'll always be a Ferguson protester," she said, but now she has taken on more of a supporting role. "I'm more so, 'If you need help, call me. If you need a sounding board, call me.' "

HE BECAME A 'SOCIAL OUTCAST IN THE ARAB COMMUNITY.'

Bassem Masri, the unofficial videographer of the Ferguson protest movement, was also one of its chief provocateurs. He won the admiration of fellow activists through his live video streams, which showed viewers — more than 10,000 on some nights — the street protests in real time.

In those streams, Mr. Masri waved his middle finger at the police and badgered shop owners armed with rifles. But amid 100 nights documenting the chaos with his iPhone, family and friends said, Mr. Masri struggled with money problems and addiction.

An Arab-American amid mostly African-American demonstrators, Mr. Masri told friends he was drawn to the protests because the unrest reminded him of demonstrations in Palestine, where his family emigrated from. And like African-Americans, Mr. Masri knew the sting of police harassment, said his friend, Faizan Syed, executive director of the Missouri chapter of the Council on American-Islamic Relations, the nation's largest Muslim civil rights organization.

Mr. Masri complained about being frequently pulled over for minor traffic violations and speeding. Those violations led to $3,000 in municipal court fees and, when he could not pay them, stints in jail, Mr. Syed said. Mr. Masri ultimately lost his driver's license.

When the protests — which had given him a sense of purpose — fizzled out, Mr. Masri became a pariah because he had supported an African-American cause that many Arab-Americans did not understand, Mr. Syed said. "He was a social outcast in the Arab community," Mr. Syed said. Soon, Mr. Masri drifted into serious drug use, even as he spoke about entering politics.

Instead, a few days after Thanksgiving in 2018, he was found dead of a fentanyl overdose on a bus. He was 31.

'I NEVER EVER IN MY WILDEST DREAMS THOUGHT I'D BE A POLITICIAN.'

After months of protesting on the streets of Ferguson, Fran Griffin could not help but be disturbed by the actions of local officials. "The people that were supposed to represent us did not," she said. "I knew that something had to be done."

Ferguson was personal for Ms. Griffin. Unlike many of the people who descended upon the streets in 2014, she had lived in the city since

FRAN GRIFFIN
WARD 3

Fran Griffin in Ferguson, Mo., in 2019.

2005, moving there to help build a better life for her children. After seeing what she felt was a slow response from city leaders, Ms. Griffin decided to dive into the political process by attending City Council meetings.

She joined a steering committee that was created to review police department policies as part of Ferguson's settlement with the Justice Department. In 2016, Ms. Griffin challenged a longtime Ferguson city councilman with a write-in campaign. She lost that race but established herself as a leader.

Ms. Griffin, 38, was one of many African-Americans to turn to politics in the aftermath of the unrest in Ferguson, but unlike many, she considers herself an activist. She challenged the incumbent again this year — as well as Michael Brown's mother, Ms. McSpadden. This time, she won.

As a councilwoman, Ms. Griffin said she was focused on amplifying the voices of those in her community. When a new Ferguson police chief was recently being hired, Ms. Griffin said, she championed a town hall in which residents got to hear from the candidates directly. "I never ever in my wildest dreams thought I'd be a politician," she said. "It definitely gave me a greater sense of responsibility to an entire community."

California Allows Public to Refuse to Help Law Enforcement

BY JACEY FORTIN | SEPT. 6, 2019

A rarely invoked state law from 1872, removed last week, had made it a misdemeanor to turn down law enforcement officials asking for help with an arrest. Here's a closer look at the history.

AFTER 147 YEARS, California residents are now free to turn down law enforcement officials who ask for help with an arrest.

A law, the California Posse Comitatus Act of 1872, had previously made it a misdemeanor, subject to a fine, for an able-bodied adult to refuse to help officials with tasks like apprehending an escaped prisoner or preventing "any breach of peace."

But the law had almost never been invoked in recent years, experts said. A bill removing it was signed by Gov. Gavin Newsom on Aug. 30, without an accompanying statement.

Here's a closer look at the history.

WHY DID THIS LAW DRAW ATTENTION NOW?

Bob Hertzberg, the Democratic state senator who sponsored the bill, said it was just a matter of cleaning up the legal code, adding that the 1872 act was "from a bygone era."

"We write so many damn laws all the time," he added. "It was time to take some off the books."

The California State Sheriffs' Association had opposed his bill. "We fear that the bill sort of discourages the notion that people should help out law enforcement if they need to be assisted," said Cory Salzillo, the association's legislative director.

But Mr. Salzillo added that he was not familiar with any modern case in which someone had been prosecuted for failing to help a law enforcement officer.

The Sacramento Bee reported on one episode in 2014 in which a county successfully cited posse comitatus in its defense in a case in which two residents of a remote town said that, after a sheriff asked them to investigate a 911 call from a neighbor, they walked in on a murder scene and were attacked.

WHAT IS 'POSSE COMITATUS'?

The Latin phrase "posse comitatus" can be translated as "force of the county." The ability of local law enforcement officials to summon civilians to keep the peace is an idea that has roots in Anglo-Saxon England.

In the United States, Southern officials invoked posse comitatus in the Fugitive Slave Act of 1850, which said that civilians could be recruited to capture people who were trying to escape from slavery.

But the phrase has also been used to prohibit federal military intervention in local affairs, as in the Posse Comitatus Act of 1878, a piece of federal legislation that is still on the books.

At the county level, posse comitatus was a way for local sheriffs to keep the peace in places where law enforcement was informal or poorly funded, as was often the case on the Western frontiers of the United States during the 1800s.

More recently, posses have helped local sheriffs to maintain order.

"They have thwarted the escapes of criminals, including serial killer Ted Bundy," wrote David B. Kopel, an author and researcher who wrote about posses for the Journal of Criminal Law and Criminology. "They also function as a citizen volunteer corps on a regular, structured basis; they assist sheriffs during county fairs, weather emergencies, and hostage situations, among many other duties."

HOW ELSE HAS IT BEEN USED?

The Posse Comitatus Act of 1878 is rife with exceptions today, but at its inception, it was essentially a way for Southern states to resist Reconstruction-era laws after they were readmitted to the Union following the Civil War, said Gautham Rao, an associate professor of history at American University and the editor of Law and History Review.

"This was basically carte blanche for Jim Crow violence," he said, adding that "the people against whom posse comitatus is often used tend to be the less empowered," such as striking workers, people considered to be politically extreme, immigrants and African Americans.

"Oftentimes it's discussed as an abstract constitutional principle, but it's always important to remember that ethnic and racial context," Dr. Rao said.

On March 7, 1965 — known as Bloody Sunday — members of a posse for the segregationist sheriff Jim Clark in Alabama joined state troopers to attack black civil rights activists who tried to cross the Edmund Pettus Bridge in Selma en route to Montgomery. In 2012, a volunteer member of a posse for Joe Arpaio, then the sheriff of Maricopa County, Ariz., accompanied a deputy on a trip to Hawaii to question officials there about Barack Obama's birth certificate.

ARE THERE ANY SIMILAR MODERN EXAMPLES?

Posses still exist, including some akin to community groups. As municipal police departments proliferated and sheriff's offices professionalized, posses increasingly lost relevance as law enforcement units.

Casey LaFrance, a law enforcement expert and associate professor at Western Illinois University, said that if there are any modern parallels to the posses of the 1800s, they might be auxiliary units or deputy reserves. Those are made up of people who undergo training to assist sheriffs' deputies in providing additional security for a community.

Militia groups, like those that stepped up activities along the United States border earlier this year in response to a surge of families migrating from Central America, including by holding some at gunpoint, would not be considered posse comitatus unless convened by a sheriff. But there do appear to be parallels between some armed vigilante groups targeting migrants today and the posses that historically targeted people fleeing enslavement, Dr. LaFrance said.

Dr. LaFrance, who said he served as a volunteer deputy in Illinois for about two years after undergoing a training program that focused mostly on handling firearms, said there were reasons to be concerned about outsourcing law enforcement work to volunteers. He pointed to reports of violence in Illinois and a fatality in Oklahoma that he thought better training could have helped prevent.

I'm a Police Chief. We Need to Change How Officers View Their Guns.

OPINION | BY BRANDON DEL POZO | NOV. 13, 2019

Why do we teach them that a person with a knife is always a lethal threat?

FEW THINGS ARE more harrowing than watching a video of a police officer confront a person in emotional crisis armed with a knife or other similar object. The officer almost always points a gun at that person and yells, "Drop it!" If staring down the barrel of a gun isn't enough to give a person pause, yelling at him or her is unlikely to make a difference.

If that person advances on the police officer, gunfire often results. Each year, American police officers shoot and kill well over 125 people armed with knives, many of them in this manner.

The public has grown impatient with seeing the same approach produce a predictably tragic result. In response, Chuck Wexler, the director of the Police Executive Research Forum, has released a guide to reducing the frequency of such incidents. At a national conference for chiefs of police in Chicago recently, he showed three videos to drive the point home: desperate people with knives met by officers who pointed guns and yelled in return.

In each case, the person grew more distressed, advanced out of a desire to be shot and was shot. Everyone suffers when this happens: the person in crisis who gets shot and may well die; the officer who will experience lifelong trauma and doubt, and his or her family and loved ones; and a community that feels it failed to help a person in need.

One of the problems is that we teach our police officers to lead with the gun. We tell officers that a knife or a shard of glass is always a lethal threat and that they should aggressively meet it with a lethal threat in return. But doing so forecloses all of the better ways to communicate with a person in crisis. There are alternatives.

Imagine being an unarmed police officer — like the ones in Iceland or Britain — in the same scenario. Barking orders as you stand there empty-handed would not only seem unnatural but also absurd. Your instincts would tell you to stay a safe distance away, try to contain the person, and calm the situation.

American police leaders can learn from their unarmed colleagues. Police academies should ingrain a wide range of skills, drills and responses in trainees before they ever handle a firearm. Training should start by sending officers into scenarios where they have to solve problems without recourse to lethal force.

Unarmed officers will cultivate an instinct to de-escalate: They will keep a safe distance, they will try to assess the true level of threat rather than see a weapon as a cue to rapidly escalate, and they will communicate in ways that reach people. There is good psychological research on what type of communication stands the best chance of calming people in distress, regardless of what is in their hands. And it is certainly not yelling at them or threatening their lives.

Only during the final phase of a police academy should trainees be presented with a firearm and taught how to use it. Officers should be taught that their weapons protect not only themselves and the public but also the life of the person who is armed and in distress, because they provide a means to stay safe if a calm and reassuring approach fails. By the end of academy, the officers will have learned that yelling at a person as you threaten to shoot is a panicked, last-ditch effort, not a sign of competence.

I lead the police force in Burlington, Vt., one of the nation's most progressive cities. One of our City Council members recently suggested that we should explore ways to disarm our city's police because it would prevent them from killing people and force them to approach crises differently.

In America, this idea is a non-starter. Police officers being rendered helpless to respond to mass shootings and other gun violence puts a community in danger. But if the police profession doesn't want politicians broaching these ideas, we owe the public a commitment to doing everything we can to respect the sanctity of life. We should fundamentally change the way police officers view their guns.

America's abhorrent rate of gun violence means that the police need the equipment and training to meet even the most lethal threats. But we have the opportunity to stop this mind-set from infecting their approach in other situations. Our nation's police departments should read Mr. Wexler's guide and take its recommendations seriously.

Going further by training officers to act as if their weapons are insurance policies, rather than persuasive devices, will transform the nation's police work. Every American will be made safer by police officers whose first instinct is to communicate with the people they encounter and whose success lies in getting the psychology of persuasion right.

BRANDON DEL POZO became the chief of police of Burlington, Vt., in 2015, after serving 19 years in the New York Police Department.

Policing: What Changed (and Didn't) Since Michael Brown Died

BY MITCH SMITH | AUG. 7, 2019

Five years after a fatal police shooting in Ferguson, Mo., began a reckoning for American policing, more officers now wear body cameras. But shootings have not slowed.

BALTIMORE — The video shows how much policing has changed. And also how much it has stayed the same.

In shaky frames recorded by a body camera, a Baltimore police sergeant chases after a man who was walking calmly away. A second officer wrestles the man to the ground and handcuffs him. The perceived offense? Criticizing the arrest of another man as he strolled by.

The encounter was another jarring display of police aggression, a topic that has prompted a national reckoning since Michael Brown, an unarmed black teenager, was fatally shot by a white police officer in Ferguson, Mo., five years ago.

Since protests in Ferguson, activists have marched in cities large and small, police chiefs have pledged sweeping reforms and new shootings in places such as Milwaukee, Cincinnati and Chicago have kept the issue in the news.

Yet for all the talk, all the promises, all the protesting, real change over the last half-decade in American policing has varied from department to department, city to city. Amid added scrutiny, deadly police shootings have continued at a steady pace, and few officers have been charged with crimes. The public's views about the police have grown increasingly divided along racial lines. And even with body cameras clipped to the chests of thousands more officers, there is often still little agreement about whether a shooting is justified.

But the recent video from Baltimore suggested that, however glacial the pace of change, law enforcement is not the same profession it was five years ago.

For one thing, the sergeant was wearing a body camera, a relatively new addition in Baltimore, where residents have long complained of police abuse. For another, it was the sergeant — not the man he chased down — who wound up being charged with a crime. And, perhaps most significant, a rank-and-file officer was seen on the video telling his superior to relax, trying to stop the situation from spiraling.

"His effort does not meet with much success, but what is significant is that this officer tried to de-escalate a seemingly unnecessary, and unnecessarily volatile, confrontation," said James K. Bredar, a federal judge overseeing court-ordered changes to the Baltimore police. "It was a positive moment — for me, the first green shoots of spring."

POLICING ON CAMERA

Dueling narratives quickly emerged after Darren Wilson, a Ferguson police officer, killed Mr. Brown, 18, on Aug. 9, 2014. Mr. Wilson said he shot to defend himself and he was cleared of criminal wrongdoing. Some witnesses disputed that version of events and called the shooting unjust.

There was one point of agreement: Video of the shooting, which did not exist, could have helped find the truth.

Since then, body cameras have become the most tangible legacy of Ferguson. In major cities and rural sheriff's offices, millions of dollars' worth of cameras were bought with great fanfare, and sometimes with federal assistance.

By 2016, nearly half of police agencies had bought body cameras. Though the devices are popular with residents and officers, they have not proved to be a cure for problems.

A study of police officers in Washington found that body cameras had little effect on behavior. In high-profile cases in Minneapolis and South Bend, Ind., officers were wearing body cameras but failed to turn them on before shooting someone. And in some instances when a body camera was recording, people still disagreed about whether a shooting was justified.

New York City police officers prepared to patrol wearing new body cameras in 2017.

A RACIAL DIVIDE

Charles Thomas, a Baltimore resident since the 1950s, watched his city turn to chaos four years ago after Freddie Gray, a young black man, died in police custody. Since then, Mr. Thomas said, relations with the police have only grown more strained.

"If they speak to me, I'll speak back," Mr. Thomas, who is black and lived near Mr. Gray, said. "But I can't say I trust one of them."

Perhaps more clearly than any other American city, Baltimore reveals how difficult it can be to change a police department. The homicide rate in Baltimore has spiked. A procession of police commissioners has come and gone. And a federal consent decree requiring an overhaul of policing is in effect.

Still, on the streets of Baltimore, black residents say their relationship with the police looks about the same — or even worse.

Since 2014, national opinions of the police have grown more polarized along racial and political lines. More white Americans and conservatives now say they have confidence in the police. More black people and liberals say they do not.

Amid that, fewer people are seeking careers in policing. Last year, a majority of chiefs surveyed said hiring had become more difficult, and two-thirds reported difficulty finding nonwhite officers.

Chuck Wexler, the executive director of the Police Executive Research Forum, which advises departments on best practices, said that drop-off in interest from highly qualified candidates could undermine progress in other areas.

"I worry about who will be the police officers of the future," he said.

MANY SHOOTINGS, FEW PROSECUTIONS

After Ferguson, police chiefs faced intense pressure to reduce the number of police shootings. Many invested in stun guns. Some departments revamped training or tightened rules on when officers could use force.

"If we see an awful thing happened somewhere else in the country, that's going right to my academy director," said Chief Ed Roessler of the Fairfax County Police Department in Virginia. "How can we prevent this from happening here? Is our policy strong enough?"

Still, police shootings have not slowed.

Since the beginning of 2015, on-duty law enforcement officers have fatally shot more than 4,400 people, or around 985 annually, with little variation from one year to the next, according to a Washington Post database that is relied on by government officials, researchers and activists. It is not clear whether those figures are higher or lower than before the Ferguson shooting because no one kept reliable data in 2014 or before.

Amid the steady pace of shootings, criminal charges against the involved officers have remained rare, and convictions rarer still. Philip Stinson, a former New Hampshire police officer who is now a professor of criminal justice at Bowling Green State University tracking manslaughter and murder charges against the police going back to 2005, said there had been no significant uptick in such prosecutions since Ferguson. Last year, he counted 10 officers arrested on murder and manslaughter charges, roughly one officer for every 100 deadly shootings.

There are, however, anecdotal signs of a small shift: Three officers were convicted of murder and sentenced to prison in the past year. Before that, Dr. Stinson had counted only one other murder conviction for an on-duty shooting since 2005.

CHANGE AND RESISTANCE

When Chris Magnus, then the police chief in Richmond, Calif., attended a protest in uniform and held a "Black Lives Matter" sign five years ago, the response from the local officers' labor union was swift condemnation.

Since Ferguson, lines have hardened between unions representing rank-and-file officers, which have mostly been skeptical of large-scale change, and police chiefs, many of whom were hired since 2014 promising change and better relations with residents.

"The harder they push, in many ways, the more of a pushback they get from the cops that work hard for them," Chief Magnus, who now leads the Tucson Police Department, said of chiefs he said he has observed across the country.

Vincent Montague Jr., a Cleveland police sergeant who leads the Black Shield, an organization of nonwhite officers, said officers have found themselves forced to re-evaluate their work and focus more on helping residents, rather than just arresting them. He said some of his colleagues who preferred the old emphasis on foot chases and drug busts had left the department.

"You weren't trained on how to better serve the community, how to be a peace officer," said Sergeant Montague, who in 2013 shot and injured a black man in downtown Cleveland, which led to a $500,000 settlement. "Now, it's more positive. You can be yourself. I became more patient and I feel like I'm more myself."

Police officers, polls have found, do not believe that the people they serve understand the complexities of their job. Some officers have spoken of a perceived war on the police, blaming unflattering news coverage and insufficiently supportive politicians for making their work more difficult.

"There's a lot of frustration within the ranks," said Lt. Bob Kroll, president of the main police union in Minneapolis.

A SHIFT IN WASHINGTON

In the first year after Mr. Brown's death, policing dominated the news.

Residents protested shootings in Milwaukee, St. Louis and Cleveland. President Barack Obama and his Justice Department responded with investigations and devastating reports of systemic failures in some cities.

But after President Trump came to office, the focus changed.

"Shifting the conversation has been a really important win," said Samuel Sinyangwe, a data scientist and activist who co-founded Campaign Zero, a group that proposes policies to reduce police shootings. "And then we saw the conversation shift back to Trump and only Trump."

As a candidate, Mr. Trump made praise for the police a staple of his rallies. As president, his administration has moved away from consent decrees, which the Obama administration used to force oversight of troubled police departments in Baltimore, Ferguson and other cities.

Christy Lopez, a former Justice Department civil rights lawyer who led federal investigations that found patterns of discriminatory policing in Ferguson and Chicago, said she feared that some places operating under consent decrees had gone into a backslide since Mr. Trump's inauguration.

But Ferguson's legacy, she said, can still be seen as police chiefs and residents in some cities have continued pushing for change, even without the threat of federal intervention.

"Ferguson was a really important moment in time: It's pre- and post-Ferguson, and people look back at that," Ms. Lopez said. "Everything does still feel like it's emanating from that event."

CHAPTER 3

Community Voices: Unrest, Innovation, Involvement

In matters of social health, it is often the spontaneous efforts of communities themselves that begin the problem-solving process. The articles in this chapter give a range of examples of community input on criminal justice. Some of these examples are carefully formulated strategies, while others are less directed mass actions. Some collaborate with existing institutions, while others opt for resistance and unrest. Each of them is relevant, providing insights into how individual communities shape justice.

Blacks Mull Call for 10,000 to Curb Violence

BY JON HURDLE | SEPT. 30, 2007

PHILADELPHIA, SEPT. 29 — The men on the corner of 16th and Page in North Philadelphia say they know what their neighborhood needs to stem the violence that has killed 306 people citywide so far this year, and that does not include putting 10,000 men on the street, as some black community leaders have proposed.

Amid the weed-strewn lots and boarded-up buildings of North Philadelphia, one of the city's toughest neighborhoods, the six men who gathered to talk, drink and play cards say the young people who pull guns and deal drugs need jobs, recreation centers, after-school programs and, most of all, parents who care for them.

"It's just going to be useless," said one, Robert Mosley Jr., 42. "As soon as those 10,000 guys go home, the drug dealers are going back out there, doing the same thing."

But others supported the initiative, saying it might help them feel better about coming out of their homes at night or allowing their children to play outside.

"It does make a lot of sense," said Cora Crawford, a 36-year-old single mother of five who lives on nearby Susquehanna Avenue. "Kids in this area are horrible. They need a positive role model in their life."

The plan to put 10,000 men on the streets for an initial period of 90 days starting late this year is the latest effort by Philadelphia's black community to curb violence that drove homicides to a nine-year high of 406 in 2006.

Groups of volunteers will be stationed on drug corners and other trouble spots in a bid to stop the shootings and other crimes that have given Philadelphia the highest homicide rate among the nation's 10 largest cities. They will not be armed, will not have powers of arrest, and will be identified only by armbands or hats during their three-hour shifts.

They will be trained in conflict resolution, and are intended to be peacekeepers and mentors rather than law enforcers. Each patrol, however, will include a police officer.

Organizers, including Police Commissioner Sylvester Johnson and the music producer Kenny Gamble, say they are open to volunteers of any ethnicity but are appealing mostly to African-Americans because some 85 percent of Philadelphia's shooting victims are black.

Commissioner Johnson, who is black, said the initiative differed from previous antiviolence campaigns in that it was driven by popular demand, rather than by the Police Department or the city government.

"I have never been involved in an initiative of this size coming from the street," he said in an interview.

Residents of North Philadelphia, from left, Robert Mosley Jr., Kirk Karrin, Otis Osborne, Salaam Wakefield and Keith Rainey. Mr. Mosley said a plan to deter crime would be "useless."

Critics say the plan will fail to meet its recruitment goals, partly because it is too closely identified with the police, who will be responsible for selecting the areas to patrol and who are distrusted in many neighborhoods.

Archye Leacock, executive director of the Institute for the Development of African-American Youth, a Philadelphia nonprofit group, said the police were overburdened by trying to control the toughest areas and so would be unable to respond adequately to alerts from the volunteers.

Mr. Leacock also questioned whether the plan would motivate a generation of people who have learned to live with crime and violence.

But Bilal Qayyum, a co-founder of the antiviolence group Men United for a Better Philadelphia and a member of the organizing committee, described the response since the plan was announced Sept.

10 as "tremendous." He predicted more than 10,000 volunteers would come forward when it starts on Oct. 21.

Mr. Qayyum conceded that the plan did not address underlying problems like unemployment, poverty, poor education and the easy availability of guns. Drug dealers will probably just move to the next block to avoid the new volunteers, he said.

But he said that getting men to take responsibility for their own communities was a step in the right direction. "That begins to address the core problem," he said.

Near 16th and Page, Tyrone Dodson, 60, expressed hope that the plan would work. Like several others, Mr. Dodson said he planned to sign up because he believed it would deter the shootings outside his apartment almost every night.

"It would stop them," he said. "They don't want no witnesses."

The Pulse: Antiviolence
Ritual From a Faraway Land

BY RACHEL CROMIDAS | AUG. 13, 2010

AFTER YEARS OF FRUSTRATION, Cheryl Graves was ready to consider a different solution to Chicago's problem of youth violence.

Ms. Graves, a community organizer, had spent more than 10 years training representatives of the intervention group Cease-Fire and administrators of violence-ridden Fenger High School in conflict-resolution techniques at the Community Justice for Youth Institute. But she felt that her efforts were meeting with more failures than successes. Many Chicago Public School students were still going to jail as a result of violent outbreaks in school. It was time to try something else.

So on Monday, Ms. Graves and her colleagues took the unusual step of going to the Maori House at the Field Museum, a sacred wood structure that the museum bought from New Zealand in 1905. There they joined South African activists working to prevent street violence in Cape Town to perform a peacekeeping ritual inspired by the Maori tradition.

The organizers said they hoped the Maori ritual, which requires opposing groups to sing and hug after exchanging speeches, could provide new insight into changing the attitudes of at-risk youths who are sometimes reluctant to resolve disputes verbally.

Ms. Graves said the point of the meeting was to address a simple question. "What can we do to not just reduce the violence, but create relationships in the communities that can withstand and prevent violence from within?" she said.

Ryan Hollon, who organized the meeting, works with CeaseFire and the Community Justice for Youth Institute and serves as an anthropologist at the museum.

"People shouldn't have to come to a museum to have a safe space to talk about tough issues," Mr. Hollon said. "That should exist in every neighborhood across the city, especially in those neighborhoods where conflict resolutions don't exist."

From Terrorizing Streets
to Making Them Safer

BY KIA GREGORY | APRIL 24, 2013

IN ITS BLUNT RETELLING of Central Harlem, the documentary opens with Dedric Hammond standing in front of a Chinese takeout restaurant near the spot where he was shot the first time. Bullets had a circular presence in his life, beginning when he was known on the streets simply as Bad News, a name he got for being a shooter.

Now Mr. Hammond, who has been shot on two occasions and has been in prison for 8 of his 34 years, goes by a much different tag: Beloved. He sees the word as a mantra in his intent to remake himself from violence personified to what the nonprofit group he works for calls a "violence interrupter." He has also become a movie star, of sorts.

On a recent afternoon, Mr. Hammond, wearing glasses and a black hooded sweatshirt and jeans, lumbered down Lenox Avenue, headed toward one of his offices at Operation Snug, an antiviolence group, at a community center near 142nd Street. His job is to respond to every episode of violence within his catchment area, which runs from 127th to 145th Street, and from St. Nicholas Avenue to Lenox Avenue, and somehow mediate before it spreads. Information comes to him from hospital workers or social media sites that someone has been jumped, or stabbed, or shot. Or is ready to shoot. Or people go directly to him because they see him as a credible force on the streets he once terrorized.

The documentary, called "Triggering Wounds," is structured around Mr. Hammond's story. It runs 15 minutes and will be screened at the Tribeca Film Festival on Thursday night, and then in a weeklong series at the Maysles Institute in Harlem.

Within the petty and punishing code of the streets, it is perhaps what Mr. Hammond did after he was shot that sets his tale apart.

With his roundish frame, broad grin, and salutations of "Sir," "Ma'am," and "God Bless," Mr. Hammond looks like an oversize kid,

Dedric Hammond, also known as Beloved, is part of the focus of a film that teenage producers in Harlem helped put together.

one who got his first gun at 13 as founder of a crew in the St. Nicholas housing complex, where he still lives.

On the day after his 23rd birthday, Mr. Hammond, a high school dropout, found himself on the other side of a barrel. He had gotten into an argument with a rival on 132nd Street near a Chinese restaurant. A friend of the rival took offense, pulled a gun from his waistband, and pumped two shots into Mr. Hammond's stomach, and another into his back. Then the gunman ran.

"I went to take another step," Mr. Hammond recalled, "and I dropped."

There were more gunshots months later as Mr. Hammond stood outside his mother's home. A gunman fired nine times, hitting him twice.

Mr. Hammond said he knew he had to do what for him was a drastic measure. He got someone to mediate with the man who shot him. And that eventually led to his current life. "The statistics for me was to get murdered or murder," he said.

"I now shake hands with the guy who shot me," he said. "I now shake hands with the guy who shot up my mother's house."

"Triggering Wounds" is like another candle in a sidewalk memorial. The documentary was produced by the Maysles Institute Teen Producers Academy, in partnership with the Manhattan district attorney's office and with Harlem Hospital Center, where it will be shown to gunshot and stabbing victims. So far this year, in the two police precincts that make up Central Harlem, there have been 2 homicides, 9 shootings and 22 recovered guns.

"It's painful," said Langston Sanchez, 18, one of the 14 student producers involved with the film. "You can feel the pain and heartbreak, and feeling of loss."

One goal, said Christine Peng, education director at the Maysles Institute, is for those involved in gun violence to "not have feelings of retaliation in the moment."

She added, "It's this back and forth that makes gun violence an epidemic in the Harlem community." She said it was also "really important for people outside the community to feel that gut-awful feeling, to feel its devastation."

The 16-month project shows those on the front lines: a police official holding a map of what he calls the battleground; a room of grieving parents, where a teary father, whose son died in his arms, said, "Sometimes I want to die"; a summit of fearful, frustrated teens; emergency responders driving through the streets; a morgue assistant wielding a buzzing saw used in autopsies; and Mr. Hammond.

"Beloved is a very powerful person," said Iesha Sekou, founder of Street Corner Resources, a community-based service organization. Ms. Sekou first met Beloved at a community meeting, when he was fresh out of prison. "When we go into a room, or enter a playground," she said, "he has a certain power over young people; they listen to him. He gets their ear very fast. That's a powerful thing."

She explained: "He's able to flex between being a person who understands the streets and why people shoot, and flip it to keep young people from shooting. It's not fake to these kids."

As Mr. Hammond made his way inside the community center, he looked across the street at about a half-dozen young men in front of a grocery store, a fixture on the corner like the stop sign. But before he can go to talk to them, or to head to St. Nicholas Houses to try to quell a gang dispute, a young woman who looked to be in her late teens stopped him, in need of his help. Because of who her friends are, when she ventures past 140th Street, he said, people are "throwing bottles at her, getting girls to beat her up, throwing shots at her area."

"It's certain areas in Harlem that kids just can't go," Mr. Hammond explained. "And if they do, they can get murdered."

A Quandary for Mexico as Vigilantes Rise

BY RANDAL C. ARCHIBOLD | JAN. 15, 2014

ANTÚNEZ, MEXICO — Word spread quickly: The army was coming to disarm the vigilante fighters whom residents viewed as conquering heroes after they swept in and drove out a drug gang that had stolen property, extorted money and threatened to kill them. They even had to leave flowers and other offerings at a shrine to the gang's messianic leader.

Farmers locked arms with vigilantes to block the dusty two-lane road leading here. The soldiers demanded to be let in; people begged them to leave. Tempers flared, and rocks were thrown. The soldiers fired into the air, and then, residents said, into a crowd. At least two people were killed on Tuesday, officials and residents said.

"He was just a farmer, and now he died for a cause," one resident, Luis Sánchez, said of Mario Torres, 48, a lime picker who was not part of the vigilante group but was among the two buried on Wednesday as mourners cried out against the government and the soldiers.

As convoys of federal police officers and soldiers crisscrossed the rolling farmland, the turmoil here in Michoacán State — where vigilantes have taken up arms to battle cartel gunmen on village streets — has confronted the image-conscious Mexican government with a thorny security challenge and a daunting Catch-22.

Should it disarm the loosely organized gunmen who have risen up to fight the drug cartels, risking deadly clashes with some of the very citizens it has been accused of failing to protect in the first place?

Or should it back down and let these nebulous outfits — with little or no police training, uncertain loyalties and possible ties to another criminal gang — continue to fight against the region's narcotics rings, possibly leading to a bloody showdown?

Here in the town where the civilians were killed, the government seems to have chosen the second option: to back off and cool down.

Relatives mourn a man killed Tuesday in Antúnez, Mexico, after soldiers moved in to disarm vigilantes. Residents view the fighters as conquering heroes.

After Mexican officials urged the vigilantes to disarm and go home, this small farming town and at least one other that resisted the government remained under the control of gunmen — some of them teenagers — in battered pickups.

The rise of the so-called self-defense groups is perhaps the most striking example of the weakness of policing, exposing a strain of vigilantism that courses through the country, especially in rural areas where frustration and a lack of confidence in institutions is deepest.

"Michoacán, and especially its western mountainous region, has suffered persistent problems of violence and perhaps a more persistent problem with the state's weak response to violence," said Matthew C. Ingram, an assistant professor at the University at Albany who studies Mexico's justice institutions. "If the state cannot or will not do it, then, in short, ordinary citizens take it upon themselves to do it."

Or, as the Rev. Antonio Mendoza, the Roman Catholic priest who presided over the funeral of the two victims here on Wednesday, put it, "the solution is legality and rule-of-law reforms."

"Until we have them," he added, "people will take justice into their own hands."

It was clear that the attempt by the government to reassert authority would come at best in fits and starts, offering little interference with the groups in some towns where they agreed to put down or at least hide their weapons, and backing off where it was not welcome. Late Wednesday, the federal government named a commissioner to direct its effort in Michoacán. In Apatzingán, a small city that the vigilantes had vowed to seize because they see it as the stronghold of the Knights Templar drug ring, federal police officers kept a heavy presence. Still, a pharmacy had been burned under suspicious circumstances, and several businesses had closed under threat by the Knights Templar, local reporters said.

Late Wednesday, the government announced the arrest of two men it called leaders of the Knights Templar, including Joaquín Negrete, who is accused of 11 murders in the region. But members of the self-defense groups told local media that the men were not top leaders and had no plans to lay down their arms.

At a meeting Wednesday night among the groups, they agreed to seek a way to work together with the federal police and little by little give up their arms, Estanislao Beltran, a spokesman for the group, told reporters afterward, according to El Universal, a newspaper.

Here in Antúnez, there were no signs of federal police officers or soldiers, and certainly no disarmament. And residents would not have it any other way.

"Since they came last week, everything changed," said a fruit vendor who, like many here, spoke in whispers and anonymously out of fear that the gang that had ruled would return. "It is peaceful."

In nearby Parácuaro, where the burned remnants of a truck and a bus left over from a clash with the gang remained, the vigilantes kept a blockade at the town's entrance.

A member of a so-called self-defense group on the streets of Antúnez, where a drug gang had held sway.

According to residents, the Knights Templar moved in a couple of years ago, erecting a shrine to its mysterious leader, Nazario Moreno González. The government says that he was killed three years ago and that his followers, who revere him with something approaching religious adoration, have forced people to leave offerings to him. Yet there have been many reports across Michoacán that Mr. Moreno González is still alive. (The Knights Templar are an offshoot of his old gang, La Familia Michoacana.)

Residents told of a long ordeal of terror and helplessness. A landowner was killed when he refused to surrender property. Trucks, money and other valuables ended up with gang leaders and their allies. And death threats became commonplace. The town police, residents said, were bought off or forced to work for the gang.

"The leader of the Knights, even when he was leaving here when the self-defense police came in, said they would be back and would kill us all," the vendor said.

The self-defense group, armed with automatic rifles and police-style pickups that it said had been seized from the gang, swept in. The group denied suggestions by some in the government that it represented another gang, the New Generation, but when questioned about how ordinary farmers could disarm vicious and hardened criminals, members declined to discuss tactics.

The local police disappeared, they said, and the gang members, outmanned, went into hiding or, perhaps, left to regroup.

The vigilantes set up a checkpoint at the entrance to Antúnez, screening visitors and receiving fruit, tacos and even small cash payments from residents, voluntarily, they insisted. They have a ragtag look to them, and some are clearly not accustomed to handling weapons. As a leader of the group spoke to a reporter, another member accidentally discharged his rifle as he got into a truck.

But it was difficult to find residents who did not appreciate them.

One of the first things the vigilantes did was destroy the image of Mr. Moreno González in the shrine's doghouse-size chapel. Residents later replaced it with a statue of the Virgin of Guadalupe, the patron saint of Mexico.

How Community Policing Can Work

OPINION | BY CHARLIE BECK AND CONNIE RICE | AUG. 12, 2016

LOS ANGELES — After the recent murders of police officers in Dallas and Baton Rouge, La., and the devastating videos of the shooting deaths of black men like Alton B. Sterling and Philando Castile, the future of police-community relations in cities all over America hangs in the balance. But even as the country is still reeling from these traumas, this is no time for despair.

Since the urban unrest of the 1960s, a series of post-riot audits — from the McCone, Kerner and Christopher Commissions to President Obama's Task Force on 21st-Century Policing (on which one of us serves) — have prescribed the same remedy for police-community conflict: move to guardian policing, overcome bias and replace the "spiral of despair" in poor neighborhoods with opportunity and justice.

We have yet to deliver on many of these — despite the regular reminders we get. Just this week, the report on Baltimore commissioned by the Department of Justice after the 2015 death in police custody of Freddie Gray prescribed a transformation of police culture and practice supervised by the courts, much like the "consent decree" imposed on the Los Angeles Police Department in 2001. At that time, the city faced a total breakdown of public-police trust; since then, we have come a long way, but reform is still a work in progress.

One of us is the chief of the Los Angeles Police Department. The other is a civil rights lawyer who, for years, sued that department. It's safe to say that the Hatfields and the McCoys shared more affection than we did. But in 2002 we joined forces with: Mayor James Hahn; a Federal District Court judge, Gary A. Feess; the chief of police at the time, William J. Bratton; and an army of reformers in an urgent quest for a police culture that no longer prompted race riots or judicial supervision.

Call it guardian policing, trust policing, problem-solving policing, relationship-based policing, community policing or partnership policing. The many names share one vision: humane, compassionate, culturally fluent cops who have a mind-set of respect, do not fear black men, and serve long enough to know residents' names, speak their languages and help improve the neighborhood.

We believed this approach could reduce bad policing, bolster law enforcement and increase public safety. We went out to prove it, and 15 years later, we think we have.

Come to Watts and East Los Angeles and you will see the Police Department's Community Safety Partnership unit, which operates in seven of the city's most violent public housing projects. Here, officers call out residents' names in greeting and patrol on foot with gang intervention specialists. The officers earn trust by participating in a range of neighborhood activities — everything from buying bifocals for older people to helping start a farmers' market and sports leagues for kids. The unit's officers are not promoted for making arrests, but for demonstrating how they diverted a kid from jail and increased trust.

Above all, they do not view residents of high-crime areas as potential suspects or deportees but as partners in public safety. In white neighborhoods, they are trained to not see black men as out-of-place threats. Many other officers, of course, strive for these goals, though they often do so without the special training and extra resources of this program.

But the police are only half the equation. This partnership demands changes from the community that may be even harder to deliver. In Los Angeles, grieving parents had to agree to join cops who had jailed or killed their children during the wars on drugs and gangs. The Community Safety Partnership began with an officer's apology for past police transgressions; after that, Watts and East Los Angeles leaders agreed to work with the Police Department in the pilot program.

The benefits are manifest. In its first year, the partnership unit posted the department's steepest crime reductions and has sustained those drops ever since. For nearly two years after the start of the program, three housing projects that had once suffered several killings a year did not have a single murder. And in Watts, there have been no shootings by the partnership officers in over five years.

The true test of guardian policing, however, is during a crisis. This is when the reservoir of trust saves lives — as it did three weeks ago, after a Los Angeles police officer killed a young man who was shooting at the police.

Angry members of the community demanded an emergency meeting with the police. At the end of the painful session, a former gang leader concluded that the death was extremely sad, but "if you shoot at the cops, you should expect to die." Other attendees handed officers rosaries, and they apologized for earlier "kill the cops" talk after rumors that officers had fired when the young man was surrendering.

In the past, there would have been no listening — bottles, rocks and worse would have been the only response. But by morning, calm had taken hold.

The same dividend for guardian policing was evident in Dallas. Despite the worst efforts of a determined, vicious assassin, community policing efforts there yielded an outpouring of public grief for the slain officers and gratitude for their service, as well as equal heartbreak over the recent police shooting deaths of black men. Since the shootings, about 500 people have applied to join the Dallas Police Department.

We have much to do before most poor neighborhoods in Los Angeles see the Police Department through a lens of trust. The Community Safety Partnership is only one unit; we need more. But it is solid evidence that this is not the last century's police department and that guardian policing is part of the solution to conflict between police and community. If it works for the housing projects of Los Angeles, it can work anywhere.

CHARLIE BECK is the chief of the Los Angeles Police Department. CONNIE RICE, a civil rights lawyer, is a member of the President's Task Force on 21st-Century Policing.

Attica, Attica: The Story of the Legendary Prison Uprising

REVIEW | BY JAMES FORMAN JR. | AUG. 30, 2016

BLOOD IN THE WATER
The Attica Prison Uprising of 1971 and Its Legacy
By Heather Ann Thompson
Illustrated. 724 pp. Pantheon Books. $35.

ATTICA. THE NAME ITSELF has long signified resistance to prison abuse and state violence. In the 1975 film "Dog Day Afternoon," Al Pacino, playing a bank robber, leads a crowd confronting the police in a chant of "Attica, Attica." The rapper Nas, in his classic "If I Ruled the World," promises to "open every cell in Attica, send 'em to Africa." And Attica posters were once commonplace in the homes of black nationalists. The one in my family's apartment in the 1970s featured a grainy black-and-white picture of Attica's protesting prisoners, underneath the words "We are not beasts."

But memories of the 1971 uprising at Attica prison have grown hazy. I recently mentioned the word to a politically active Yale College student, who responded: "I know it's a prison where something important happened. But I'm not sure of the details."

Heather Ann Thompson, a professor of history at the University of Michigan, has the details. Thompson spent more than a decade poring over trial transcripts, issuing countless requests for hidden government documents, and interviewing dozens of survivors and witnesses. The result is "Blood in the Water," a masterly account of the Attica prison uprising, its aftermath and the decades-long legal battles for justice and accountability. This is not an easy book to read — the countless episodes of inhumanity on these pages are heartbreaking. But it is an essential one.

Isolated in the far western corner of New York State (Attica is closer to Detroit than to New York City, where almost half of its prisoners come from), the prison in 1971 housed nearly 2,300 men who were permitted only one shower a week and provided a single roll of toilet paper each month ("one sheet per day," went the saying). Men regularly went to bed hungry, as the state spent just 63 cents per prisoner per day for food. Puerto Rican prisoners suffered special discrimination; prisoner mail was censored, and since corrections officers couldn't read Spanish, they simply tossed those letters in the trash. Black prisoners had it worst of all, as they were relegated to the lowest-paid jobs and racially harassed by the prison's almost all-white staff.

Drawing strength from the civil rights activism of the era, Attica's prisoners lobbied to improve their living conditions. But all they got were vague, unfulfilled promises. After months of mounting tensions, on Sept. 9, 1971, a group of prisoners saw a chance to overpower an officer. The Attica riot was underway.

Among the riot's first casualties was Correction Officer William Quinn, who was beaten so badly that he was almost unrecognizable to a paramedic who had known him for years. (Quinn would die days later.) But after a few hours of bloody chaos, a group of inmate leaders emerged to restore order. One of their first public statements came from L.D. Barkley, whose plain-spoken claim to humanity would inspire posters like the one in our apartment. "We are men," Barkley said. "We are not beasts, and we do not intend to be beaten or driven as such."

Prison leaders quickly sought to negotiate with Gov. Nelson Rockefeller and other state officials, conditioning their surrender on the granting of 33 demands. These included better education, less mail censorship, more religious freedom, fairer disciplinary and parole processes and, most controversially, amnesty for crimes committed in the course of the riot itself.

Negotiations were led by a group of journalists, politicians and prison reformers, including the radical civil rights attorney William Kunstler and the New York Times columnist Tom Wicker. Shuttling between prisoners in the yard and state authorities gathered outside, the negotiators worked heroically toward a settlement. But Rockefeller was uncompromising, and after refusing to go to Attica to join the negotiations himself, he abandoned talks and ordered state troopers to "retake" the prison.

I wouldn't have thought that Rockefeller — the sponsor of reviled mandatory drug sentences bearing his name — could suffer any more damage to his reputation on criminal justice matters. But Thompson methodically shreds him, depicting a craven politician thoroughly uninterested in the human consequences of his decisions.

The savagery that followed the decision to retake the prison was both predictable and avoidable. The prisoners had no guns themselves, yet the troopers — untrained, unsupervised and out for vengeance — began shooting wildly upon entering. Among the first to die were corrections officers held as hostages, as well as the prisoners who had been guarding them. Thirty-nine people — 29 prisoners and 10 hostages — would be killed.

The most sadistic crimes took place after state officials had full control of the prison. Prisoners were forced to strip naked and run through a gantlet of 30 to 40 corrections officers who took turns beating them with batons. One National Guardsman described seeing a gravely injured black man being attacked by a corrections officer. "They forced him to his knees, and at that point, the correction sergeant backed up a short distance and then ran forward and kicked the man in the face. ... He immediately went limp and his head was hanging down, he was bleeding." Another Guardsman recalled watching medical staff join in the abuse. He saw a doctor "speaking to the inmates and saying: 'You say you're hurt? You're not hurt. We'll see if you're hurt.' " Instead of attending to their wounds, the doctor began kicking and hitting them.

There are dozens more harrowing tales like these. And then there are the photographs, some depicting naked and abused prisoners, marched for sport before sullen, leering guards. Eventually I had to put the book down. To breathe. To wipe the tears. I couldn't stop thinking of slave narratives. Or of Ta-Nehisi Coates's claim that "in America, it is traditional to destroy the black body — it is heritage."

Thompson dwells on these stories because she wants us to learn, and then never forget, what the state of New York tried to hide. The truth of what happened in that prison yard 45 years ago has been suppressed by flagrant lies (including Rockefeller's claim that the prisoners, not his own troopers, had killed the hostages), unwarranted secrecy (the state still refuses to release thousands of boxes of crucial records), and cover-ups (when a prosecutor got close to indicting some of the state troopers for their role in the killings, his superiors stopped him from going forward).

"Blood in the Water" comes out at an important time. Criminal justice reform is having something of a moment. But Thompson's tale is a cautionary reminder that we've been here before. The Attica uprising took place in the midst of an earlier period of activism, and had the potential to be a turning point toward better prison conditions. When these mostly black and brown men took over the yard and asked for things like better education, the state could have recognized the legitimacy of their demands. Instead they were slaughtered, the crime was concealed, and in the decades since, America has shown little regard for prisoner welfare.

But Attica's tragic outcome doesn't undermine the significance of the resistance. As Thompson argues: "The Attica uprising of 1971 happened because ordinary men, poor men, disenfranchised men, and men of color had simply had enough of being treated as less than human. That desire, and their fight, is by far Attica's most important legacy." Just so, and "Blood in the Water" restores their struggle to its rightful place in our collective memory.

JAMES FORMAN JR. is a professor at Yale Law School. His "Locking Up Our Own: Crime and Punishment in Black America" will be published next spring.

The Secret Behind the Viral Churro Seller Video

BY ANDREA SALCEDO | NOV. 18, 2019

A grass-roots criminal justice organization, Decolonize This Place, has become a clearinghouse for videos of police behavior on the subway.

SOFIA B. NEWMAN, an actress with about 2,500 Twitter followers, was returning home from work this month when she saw a woman who was selling churros at the Broadway Junction subway station in Brooklyn having a heated discussion with four police officers.

Ms. Newman said she started recording the interaction with her phone so she would have evidence in case it escalated.

"The moment I saw four officers surrounding a woman of color, it was a red flag for me," Ms. Newman, 23, said.

She posted the video, which shows the vendor being handcuffed, on her Twitter account at 12:30 a.m. and then went to sleep.

By the morning, the post had received nearly 50 retweets, mostly from friends and relatives, she said.

But Ms. Newman also received a message from Decolonize This Place, a grass-roots criminal justice organization. The group asked if it could post her video on its Twitter and Instagram accounts, along with a narrative of the arrest. She agreed.

And that's when "it started blowing up," Ms. Newman said.

As of Sunday, the post had been retweeted 11,300 times and had been liked by almost 25,000 people.

Within days of the altercation, several local officials, including Eric Adams, the Brooklyn borough president, and Corey Johnson, the City Council speaker, two Democrats who are expected to run for mayor in 2021, had seen the video and criticized the officers' behavior.

It was just the latest in a series of videos, which have been viewed millions of times on Twitter, that have outraged many New Yorkers and resurfaced a conversation about police officers' interactions with civilians on the subway at a time when Gov. Andrew M. Cuomo, a Democrat, is pushing for 500 more officers to be hired at a cost of nearly $250 million to patrol the transit system.

These videos have all followed a similar pattern: They were recorded by bystanders who happened to be in the subway when the encounters happened, and who in most cases had few followers on social media. Yet they attracted a lot of attention almost immediately after being posted.

The common denominator? They all gained prominence after being promoted on the social media accounts of Decolonize This Place.

Amin Husain and Marz Saffore, co-organizers of Decolonize, said the videos showed a reality that people of color had experienced for decades. "Now the argument can't be made that this is a one-time incident," Mr. Husain, 44, said.

The videos have put the Police Department on the defensive, demonstrating the power of social media and the role technology now has in holding law enforcement accountable. The police say civilians are focusing on the wrong people: Politicians are the ones who can affect the economic conditions that often result in people with limited opportunities loitering in the subway or selling food there illegally, they say.

"A lot of elected officials came out and their immediate reaction was to criticize the N.Y.P.D.," Police Commissioner James P. O'Neill said of the churro vendor video at a news conference on Thursday. "I'd like to see a time when their first reaction is to help the woman that was selling churros."

"It's good that people see this," he added, referring to the viral videos. "Being a cop anywhere is a tough job, and we need the cooperation from all 8.6 million New Yorkers."

The phenomenon of videos of police behavior becoming viral is nothing new. In the past six years, footage captured by cellphones and police body cameras have prompted protests and started a national conversation on the role race plays in policing and the excessive use of force.

The difference in New York is that one organization, Decolonize This Place, has become the clearinghouse and gatekeeper for most of these videos.

Decolonize, founded in 2016, has 10 members and works with more than 50 other grass-roots organizations, Mr. Husain said. Its Instagram account has over 86,000 followers, and its Twitter account has nearly 11,000.

Since late October, when Decolonize posted the video of an officer punching two teenagers on the subway and another one depicting officers swarming into a subway car to arrest a man, Mr. Husain said people had been sending the organization about 10 videos a day. Staff members are also on the lookout for videos to post, as they did in the case of the churro vendor.

But his organization cannot post all of the videos it receives, Mr. Husain said. Five staff members who handle the group's social media accounts — two of whom are pursuing advanced degrees in media studies — scrutinize the videos to see which ones might have the biggest reach.

The staff members make sure that a video is accurate and that they have enough context of the incident, Mr. Husain said. They also work to ensure that it does not depict a subway incident the group has previously brought to light.

Decolonize also avoids sharing videos that show people being beaten out of respect for the victim, Mr. Husain said. The organization says it asks for permission to use each video and has never paid for any content.

"It's the combination of thinking about the Instagram account, about the content we put out, about the movement and the moment what makes these videos blow up," he said. "It's connected to on-the-ground organizing."

Days before Ms. Newman recorded the churro vendor's arrest, Erin Quinlan, a freelance journalist based in New York, recorded two officers asking a man to leave the First Avenue station in Manhattan.

Ms. Quinlan, 40, said the tone of the conversation raised a "red flag" and pushed her to record it.

In the video, she can be heard repeatedly asking why the officers are trying to remove the man; they do not respond. An officer can be seen telling Ms. Quinlan: "Why don't you mind your own business? It seems like you are looking for a lawsuit."

Ms. Quinlan posted the video on her Instagram account the next morning and tagged Decolonize. At that point, it had been viewed only about 100 times, Ms. Quinlan said.

"I intentionally wanted them to see it," Ms. Quinlan, who has about 450 Instagram followers, said of Decolonize, which received her permission to share the video.

It has now been viewed over 400,000 times, and has more than 19,000 likes and 900 comments on Decolonize's Instagram account.

Without the organization's help, she said, "there's no question almost no one would have seen it."

On Tuesday, another video of an arrest of a subway vendor went viral after it was shared by Decolonize.

The footage shows four police officers piling on top of a man on the subway platform at the 125th Street station in East Harlem. The Police Department later said the man, identified as Byron Shark, 26, had been selling candy illegally.

"When the officers attempted to take him into custody, he would not cooperate and refused to allow them to handcuff him," the department said in a statement. "As a result, officers assisted in removing the individual from the platform, and the individual eventually walked on his own accord."

Mr. Shark was arrested on charges of obstructing governmental administration and violating a local law.

On Twitter, that video has been viewed 488,000 times, and it has garnered 750 retweets and almost 1,500 likes.

Ms. Quinlan said her video had become so popular that she could not keep up with the hundreds of comments and direct messages she had received from supporters as well as critics. In the end, she said, she wished she had never been in a situation that required her to take out her phone.

"It's not about Go! Yay bystanders!" Ms. Quinlan said. "It's about what can we do to safeguard the most vulnerable of the community. I want no need for bystanders or good Samaritans."

MICHAEL GOLD contributed reporting.

ANDREA SALCEDO is a reporter for the Metro desk, and part of the 2019 New York Times Fellowship class.

CHAPTER 4

An Alternative Is Tested: Restorative Justice in Action

Recently, restorative justice programs have been introduced in schools, correctional facilities and other venues. The practice emphasizes open discussion between victim and offender in order to facilitate social healing. Along with the community-led initiatives of the last chapter, restorative justice draws on indigenous and rehabilitative models of justice.

This Penal Colony Learned a Lesson

BY CLYDE H. FARNSWORTH | AUG. 10, 1997

ALICE SPRINGS, AUSTRALIA — Between 1788 and 1868, some 160,000 British convicts — men, women, even children — stepped ashore into the prison colony of Australia, their fetters clanking down the gangways.

To British governments of the day, "transportation" was fitting punishment for the crimes, mainly against property, brought on by the miseries of the industrial revolution. Not only would hard labor in the antipodes eliminate what was seen as a burgeoning criminal class, its threat would deter any innocents who might be tempted to ease the trials of poverty by thievery. Redemption of the criminal barely figured in government thinking.

It was a cruel system. Some convicts were treated brutally. Many died under appalling conditions. And the punishment hardly worked as a deterrent. Crime continued apace in the mother country.

Yet as Robert Hughes observed in his history "The Fatal Shore," what emerged "represents by far the most successful form of penal rehabilitation that had ever been tried in English, American or European history." Convicts could not only work their way back to freedom, but with a "ticket of leave" could become butchers, farmers and mechanics. With a labor shortage in the colony, there was far more opportunity than in Britain. Fortunes could be made.

If Australians once felt ashamed of their convict past, they slowly came to see it as a source of pride; so highly do they value the redemptive aspects of the penal colony that their $20 note features Mary Reibey, who was transported as a 13-year-old orphan and horse thief but became Australia's first successful businesswoman.

ROOM TO EXPERIMENT

Today Australia continues at the cutting edge of restorative justice. With its more lenient sentencing policies, 30-year-old ban on capital punishment and accent on rehabilitation, it is in the same progressive league as Canada and the countries of northern Europe. But it is the leader of a system known as diversionary conferencing, which originated in New Zealand, based on Maori practice, and was formalized here as an alternative to traditional justice.

"We're a settler society," said Robert Manne, editor of Quadrant, a monthly political and literary review, and an associate professor of politics at La Trobe University. "The lack of rootedness of the older society allows the possibility of experimentation."

Mr. Hughes, who has lived in the United States for 30 years but visits his native country one month a year, described the Australian way of justice as "certainly the civilized way of doing it, as opposed to the barbarism of the United States."

The idea of diversionary conferencing is to let the people affected by a crime, usually families of both victims and offenders, together determine how to repair the damage, mete out punishment and minimize further harm. If guilt is confessed, the police may offer the conferencing option, which both reduces the burden on the courts and tends to work more in favor of the victim.

One study by Heather Strang, a research fellow in law at the Australian National University, and Lawrence W. Sherman, head of the criminology department of the University of Maryland, found that when conferencing took place, victims became much more likely to receive an apology from the offender (74 percent) than if the offender was sent to court (11 percent).

BETTER IMAGE, BETTER RESULTS

With conferencing victims were 10 times more likely to receive some form of repair — whether money, services or other compensation — for the harm of the crime (83 percent) than victims whose cases were assigned to court (8 percent).

"The police themselves are in a no-loss situation," said Senior Sergeant Don Fry of the Alice Springs police force. "We're improving our image and relationship both with victims and offenders."

All Australian states and territories operate some conferencing programs; experiments are under way elsewhere, including Singapore and, in the United States, in Pennsylvania, Minnesota and South Dakota.

"We haven't found any evidence it's not working," said John Braithwaite, a law professor at Australian National University. "This is the kind of criminal justice people can relate to."

The practice especially relates to Australia's Aborigines, said Lorraine Liddle, the first Aboriginal lawyer in central Australia and the lead lawyer at the Central Australian Legal Aid Service in Alice Springs.

Aborigines represent 20 percent of Alice Springs' population but 95 percent of the arrests. "In court the Aborigine feels everyone is against him," Ms. Liddle said. "The justice system is a mystery. It's imposed from somewhere else. If you negotiate something with the parents or elders that keeps the offender out of the courts and invokes traditional laws, that's very powerful."

One recent conference dealt with two 15-year-old boys, one of them Aboriginal, who after a night of drinking did $6,000 worth of damage to Alice Springs High School.

"When you arrive at school in the morning and see vandalism like that, you get mad," said the school principal, Donald L. Zoellner. But he found that both families were tougher on the boys than he thought was warranted. The restitution that everyone agreed on was to work 100 hours together helping to improve the school grounds.

"We're a small, isolated community," Mr. Zoellner said. "These kids, particularly the Aboriginal kids, are going to be here for the rest of their lives. While there's a place for detention, if we can do something that takes a longer-term view and keeps them part of a functioning system, that's just a whole lot better for everybody."

Can Forgiveness Play a Role in Criminal Justice?

BY PAUL TULLIS | JAN. 4, 2013

AT 2:15 IN THE AFTERNOON on March 28, 2010, Conor McBride, a tall, sandy-haired 19-year-old wearing jeans, a T-shirt and New Balance sneakers, walked into the Tallahassee Police Department and approached the desk in the main lobby. Gina Maddox, the officer on duty, noticed that he looked upset and asked him how she could help. "You need to arrest me," McBride answered. "I just shot my fiancée in the head." When Maddox, taken aback, didn't respond right away, McBride added, "This is not a joke."

Maddox called Lt. Jim Montgomery, the watch commander, to her desk and told him what she had just heard. He asked McBride to sit in his office, where the young man began to weep.

About an hour earlier, at his parents' house, McBride shot Ann Margaret Grosmaire, his girlfriend of three years. Ann was a tall 19-year-old with long blond hair and, like McBride, a student at Tallahassee Community College. The couple had been fighting for 38 hours in person, by text message and over the phone. They fought about the mundane things that many couples might fight about, but instead of resolving their differences or shaking them off, they kept it up for two nights and two mornings, culminating in the moment that McBride shot Grosmaire, who was on her knees, in the face. Her last words were, "No, don't!"

Friends couldn't believe the news. Grosmaire was known as the empathetic listener of her group, the one in whom others would confide their problems, though she didn't often reveal her own. McBride had been selected for a youth-leadership program through the Tallahassee Chamber of Commerce and was a top student at Leon High School, where he and Grosmaire met. He had never been in any serious trouble. Rod Durham, who taught Conor and Ann in theater classes and was close to both, told me that when he saw "Conor shot Ann" in a text message, "I was like: 'What? Is there another Conor and Ann?' "

At the police station, Conor gave Montgomery the key to his parents' house. He had left Ann, certain he had killed her, but she was still alive, though unresponsive, when the county sheriff's deputies and police arrived.

THAT NIGHT, Andy Grosmaire, Ann's father, stood beside his daughter's bed in the intensive-care unit of Tallahassee Memorial Hospital. The room was silent except for the rhythmic whoosh of the ventilator keeping her alive. Ann had some brainstem function, the doctors said, and although her parents, who are practicing Catholics, held out hope, it was clear to Andy that unless God did "wondrous things," Ann would not survive her injuries. Ann's mother, Kate, had gone home to try to get some sleep, so Andy was alone in the room, praying fervently over his daughter, "just listening," he says, "for that first word that may come out."

Ann's face was covered in bandages, and she was intubated and unconscious, but Andy felt her say, "Forgive him." His response was immediate. "No," he said out loud. "No way. It's impossible." But Andy kept hearing his daughter's voice: "Forgive him. Forgive him."

Ann, the last of the Grosmaires' three children, was still living at home, and Conor had become almost a part of their family. He lived at their house for several months when he wasn't getting along with his own parents, and Andy, a financial regulator for the State of Florida, called in a favor from a friend to get Conor a job. When the police told Kate her daughter had been shot and taken to the hospital, her immediate reaction was to ask if Conor was with her, hoping he could comfort her daughter. The Grosmaires fully expected him to be the father of their grandchildren. Still, when Andy heard his daughter's instruction, he told her, "You're asking too much."

Conor's parents were in Panama City, a hundred miles away, on a vacation with their 16-year-old daughter, when they got the call from the Tallahassee Police. Michael McBride, a database administrator for the Florida Department of Transportation, and Julie, his wife, who teaches art in elementary school, knew one of them would need to stay with Conor's sister, Katy, who is developmentally disabled. It was decided that Michael would drive to Tallahassee alone.

"I put the car in reverse" to pull out of the driveway, Michael told me, "and the last thing Julie said to me was: 'Go to the hospital. Go to the hospital.' " At the freeway on-ramp, he says he thought he should stop to throw up first. He had to pull over and vomit five more times before arriving at Tallahassee Memorial.

The hallway outside Ann's room was "absolutely packed with people," and Michael became overwhelmed, feeling "like a cartoon character, shrinking." During the drive, he hadn't thought about what he would actually do when he got to the hospital, and he had to take deep breaths to stave off nausea and lean against the wall for support. Andy approached Michael and, to the surprise of both men, hugged him. "I can't tell you what I was thinking," Andy says. "But what I told him was how I felt at that moment."

"Thank you for being here," Andy told Michael, "but I might hate you by the end of the week."

"I knew that we were somehow together on this journey," Andy says now. "Something had happened to our families, and I knew being together rather than being apart was going to be more of what I needed."

Four days later, Ann's condition had not improved, and her parents decided to remove her from life support. Andy says he was in the hospital room praying when he felt a connection between his daughter and Christ; like Jesus on the cross, she had wounds on her head and hand. (Ann had instinctually reached to block the gunshot, and lost fingers.) Ann's parents strive to model their lives on those of Jesus and St. Augustine, and forgiveness is deep in their creed. "I realized it was not just Ann asking me to forgive Conor, it was Jesus Christ," Andy recalls. "And I hadn't said no to him before, and I wasn't going to start then. It was just a wave of joy, and I told Ann: 'I will. I will.' " Jesus or no Jesus, he says, "what father can say no to his daughter?"

When Conor was booked, he was told to give the names of five people who would be permitted to visit him in jail, and he put Ann's mother Kate on the list. Conor says he doesn't know why he did so — "I was in a state of shock" — but knowing she could visit put a burden on Kate. At first she didn't want to see him at all, but that feeling turned to willingness and then to a need. "Before this happened, I loved Conor," she says. "I knew that if I defined Conor by that one moment — as a murderer — I was defining my daughter as a murder victim. And I could not allow that to happen."

She asked her husband if he had a message for Conor. "Tell him I love him, and I forgive him," he answered. Kate told me: "I wanted to be able to give him the same message. Conor owed us a debt he could never repay. And releasing him from that debt would release us from expecting that anything in this world could satisfy us."

Visitors to Leon County Jail sit in a row of chairs before a reinforced-glass partition, facing the inmates on the other side — like the familiar setup seen in movies. Kate took the seat opposite Conor, and he immediately told her how sorry he was. They both sobbed, and Kate told him what she had come to say. All during that emotional quarter of an hour, another woman in the visiting area had been loudly berating an inmate, her significant other, through the glass. After Conor and Kate "had had our moment," as Kate puts it, they both found the woman's screaming impossible to ignore. Maybe it was catharsis after the tears or the need to release an unbearable tension, but the endless stream of invective somehow struck the two of them as funny. Kate and Conor both started to laugh. Then Kate went back to the hospital to remove her daughter from life support.

"UNFORTUNATELY I HAVE a lot of experience talking to the parents of dead people," says Jack Campbell, the Leon County assistant state attorney who handles many of North Florida's high-profile murder cases.

Sheriff's deputies who were investigating the case told Campbell that the Grosmaires' feelings toward the accused were unusual, but Campbell was not prepared for how their first meeting, two months after Ann's death, would change the course of Conor's prosecution.

Campbell had charged Conor with first-degree murder, which, as most people in Florida understand it, carries a mandatory life sentence or, potentially, the death penalty. He told the Grosmaires that he wouldn't seek capital punishment, because, as he told me later, "I didn't have aggravating circumstances like prior conviction, the victim being a child or the crime being particularly heinous and the like."

As he always does with victims' families, he explained to the Grosmaires the details of the criminal-justice process, including the little-advertised fact that the state attorney has broad discretion to depart from the state's mandatory sentences. As the representative of the state and the person tasked with finding justice for Ann, he could reduce charges and seek alternative sentences. Technically, he told the Grosmaires, "if I wanted to do five years for manslaughter, I can do that."

Kate sat up straight and looked at Campbell. "What?" she asked. Campbell, believing she had misunderstood and thought he was suggesting that Conor serve a prison term of just five years, tried to reassure her. "No, no," he said. "I would never do that." It was just an example of how much latitude Florida prosecutors have in a murder case.

What Campbell didn't realize was that the Grosmaires didn't want Conor to spend his life in prison. The exchange in Campbell's office turned their understanding of Conor's situation upside down and gave them an unexpected challenge to grapple with. "It was easy to think, Poor Conor, I wouldn't want him to spend his life in prison, but he's going to have to," Kate says. "Now Jack Campbell's telling me he doesn't have to. So what are you going to do?"

"He's so sorry he said that," Kate says now, of Campbell. "I mean, it opened the door for us."

MOST MODERN JUSTICE systems focus on a crime, a lawbreaker and a punishment. But a concept called "restorative justice" considers harm done and strives for agreement from all concerned — the victims, the offender and the community — on making amends. And it allows victims, who often feel shut out of the prosecutorial process, a way to be heard and participate. In this country, restorative justice takes a number of forms, but perhaps the most prominent is restorative-justice diversion. There are not many of these programs — a few exist on the margins of the justice system in communities like Baltimore, Minneapolis and Oakland, Calif. — but, according to a University of Pennsylvania study in 2007, they have been effective at reducing recidivism. Typically, a facilitator meets separately with the accused and the victim, and if both are willing to meet face to face without animosity and the offender is deemed willing and able to complete restitution, then the case shifts out of the adversarial legal system and into a parallel restorative-justice process. All parties — the offender, victim, facilitator and law enforcement — come together in a forum sometimes called a restorative-community conference. Each person speaks, one at a time and without interruption, about the crime and its effects, and the participants come to a consensus about how to repair the harm done.

The methods are mostly applied in less serious crimes, like property offenses in which the wrong can be clearly righted — stolen property returned, vandalized material replaced. The processes are designed to be flexible enough to handle violent crime like assault, but they are rarely used in those situations. And no one I spoke to had ever heard of restorative justice applied for anything as serious as murder.

The Grosmaires had learned about restorative justice from Allison DeFoor, an Episcopal priest who works as a chaplain in the Florida prison system (and before that worked as a sheriff, public defender, prosecutor and judge). Andy, who is studying to become a deacon, heard about DeFoor from a church friend and turned to him for guidance. When Andy told DeFoor that he wanted to help the accused, DeFoor suggested he look into restorative justice. "The problem,"

DeFoor says, "was the whole system was not designed to do any of what the Grosmaires were wanting." He considered restorative justice — of any kind, much less for murder — impossible in a law-and-order state. "We are nowhere near ready for this in Florida right now," DeFoor told me. "Most people would go, 'Huh?' And most conservatives would go, 'Ew.' " But as a man of the cloth, he said he believed there was always hope. He suggested the families "find the national expert on restorative justice and hire him."

By midsummer, Andy Grosmaire was meeting Michael McBride regularly for lunch. He knew that, in a way, the McBrides had lost a child, too. At one of these lunches, he told Michael about restorative justice. Maybe this could be a way to help Conor. Julie McBride, who wasn't sleeping much anyway, started spending late nights online looking for the person who might be able to help them change their son's fate. Her research led her to Sujatha Baliga, a former public defender who is now the director of the restorative-justice project at the National Council on Crime and Delinquency in Oakland.

Baliga was born and raised in Shippensburg, Pa., the youngest child of Indian immigrants. From as far back as Baliga can remember, she was sexually abused by her father. In her early teens, Baliga started dying her hair blue and cutting herself. She thought she hated herself because of her outcast status in her community, in which she was one of the few nonwhite children in her school. But then, at age 14, two years before her father died of a heart attack, she fully realized the cause of her misery: what her father had been doing was terribly wrong.

Despite the torments of her childhood, Baliga excelled in school. As an undergraduate at Harvard-Radcliffe, she was fairly certain she wanted to become a prosecutor and lock up child molesters. After college, she moved to New York and worked with battered women. When her boyfriend won a fellowship to start a school in Mumbai, she decided to follow him while waiting to hear if she had been accepted at law school.

Baliga had been in therapy in New York, but while in India she had what she calls "a total breakdown." She remembers thinking, Oh, my

God, I've got to fix myself before I start law school. She decided to take a train to Dharamsala, the Himalayan city that is home to a large Tibetan exile community. There she heard Tibetans recount "horrific stories of losing their loved ones as they were trying to escape the invading Chinese Army," she told me. "Women getting raped, children made to kill their parents — unbelievably awful stuff. And I would ask them, 'How are you even standing, let alone smiling?' And everybody would say, 'Forgiveness.' And they're like, 'What are you so angry about?' And I told them, and they'd say, 'That's actually pretty crazy.' " The family that operated the guesthouse where Baliga was staying told her that people often wrote to the Dalai Lama for advice and suggested she try it. Baliga wrote something like: "Anger is killing me, but it motivates my work. How do you work on behalf of oppressed and abused people without anger as the motivating force?"

She dropped the letter off at a booth by the front gate to the Dalai Lama's compound and was told to come back in a week or so. When she did, instead of getting a letter, Baliga was invited to meet with the Dalai Lama, the winner of the 1989 Nobel Peace Prize, privately, for an hour.

He gave her two pieces of advice. The first was to meditate. She said she could do that. The second, she says, was "to align myself with my enemy; to consider opening my heart to them. I laughed out loud. I'm like: 'I'm going to law school to lock those guys up! I'm not aligning myself with anybody.' He pats me on the knee and says, 'O.K., just meditate.' "

Baliga returned to the United States and signed up for an intensive 10-day meditation course. On the final day, she had a spontaneous experience, not unlike Andy Grosmaire's at his daughter's deathbed, of total forgiveness of her father. Sitting cross-legged on an easy chair in her home in Berkeley, Calif., last winter, she described the experience as a "complete relinquishment of anger, hatred and the desire for retribution and revenge."

After law school at the University of Pennsylvania, Baliga clerked for a federal judge in Vermont. "That's when I first saw restorative justice in action," she says. The second part of the Dalai Lama's prescription would be fulfilled after all.

EARLY IN 2011, Julie McBride called Baliga, who patiently explained why restorative justice wasn't going to happen for her son. "This is a homicide case," Baliga told Julie, "it's in the Florida panhandle, we don't know anybody who does this level of victim-offender dialogue, and I don't think there even is victim-offender dialogue in Florida, period. Just forget it. This is never going to happen."

"We want to hire you," Julie insisted.

"We do burglaries, robberies," Baliga protested. "No gun charges, no homicides. No rape. There's no way. There's never been a murder case that's gone through restorative justice."

But Julie wouldn't let it go. "I think you'll just fall in love with the Grosmaires," she told Baliga. "You just need to talk to them."

"I'm not going to cold-call them," Baliga responded.

"Oh, no, no," Julie said. "*They* told me about restorative justice. They want all this to happen. I'm just doing the legwork because they lost their daughter."

"O.K. So wait, what? You're *talking* to them?"

Baliga says she thought that Julie McBride was maybe a little deluded, traumatized, as she must have been, by what her son had done. She agreed to speak with the Grosmaires only if they called her, and within minutes of hanging up with Julie, her phone rang. Kate was on the other end.

Kate told her how Conor almost immediately turned himself in, and about Michael's coming to the hospital before going to see his son in jail. At first, Baliga says, "I had mistrust of the potential for people to be this amazing." After a few minutes of talking with them, though, she says, "I just couldn't keep saying no."

A conference call was quickly arranged that included the McBrides, the Grosmaires, Baliga, DeFoor and Conor's lawyer, a capital-crime specialist named Greg Cummings. Baliga was asking questions, trying to figure out how her diversion process might work in Florida, where nothing like it existed.

Then DeFoor had an idea: "What about the pre-plea conference?" Right away the lawyers knew this could work. A pre-plea conference is a meeting between the prosecutor and the defendant's lawyer at which a plea deal is worked out to bring to a judge. Anyone can attend, it's off the record and nothing said can be used in court. All of those conditions would also fulfill the requirements of a restorative-justice community conference.

The only obstacle that remained — and everyone knew it was a big one — was the prosecutor, Jack Campbell.

The Grosmaires' request was not without risk to Campbell. He is ambitious and approving an alternative-justice process brought by a woman from California that might result in a murderer receiving a lighter sentence would most likely make him appear soft on crime. On the other hand, "opposing a church deacon asking for mercy for his daughter's murderer has its own problems," DeFoor says. "But the safe course was for Jack Campbell to say 'no.' The circumstances did not lend themselves to him being bold."

Campbell did his own research, and once satisfied that the conference wouldn't violate his oath or, he says, "the duty I owed to every other parent and every other child in this town," he called Cummings, Conor's lawyer, whom he knew and respected, to work out the details. Campbell told Cummings that he would not necessarily abide by whatever wishes the other parties had regarding sentencing. "Just because I'm participating," he told Cummings, "doesn't mean I'm going to sign off on the product of this meeting."

THE DAY OF the conference, June 22, 2011, was hot and humid. Baliga and the Grosmaires arrived first at the small room inside Leon County Jail where the meeting would take place. Baliga felt it important that Ann be represented at the conference, so while she arranged the molded plastic chairs in a circle, the Grosmaires placed a number of Ann's belongings in the center of the room: a blanket Ann's best friend had crocheted for her; the Thespian of the Year trophy she won during senior year; a plaster cast of Ann's uninjured hand. After the McBrides, the lawyers, a victims' advocate and the Grosmaires' priest, the Rev. Mike Foley, from the Good Shepherd Catholic Church, arrived, Baliga asked the jailers to bring in Conor.

Kate and Julie rose from their chairs. Conor stood awkwardly, not sure where to go or what to do. "Conor," Baliga said, "go hug your mother." Jail policy is that there be no physical contact between inmates and visitors, but Baliga had persuaded the sheriff to make an exception. He had not touched his parents in 15 months. He hugged them and then turned to the Grosmaires. Kate and Andy had continued to visit Conor periodically — Kate particularly wanted to be with him on Ann's birthday. Now, he hugged them, too.

Baliga laid out the ground rules: Campbell would read the charges and summarize the police and sheriff's reports; next the Grosmaires would speak; then Conor; then the McBrides; and finally Foley, representing the community. No one was to interrupt. Baliga showed a picture of Ann, sticking out her tongue as she looks at the camera. If her parents heard anything Ann wouldn't like, they would hold up the picture to silence the offending party. Everyone seemed to feel the weight of what was happening. "You could feel her there," Conor told me.

The Grosmaires spoke of Ann, her life and how her death affected them. "We went from when she was being born all the way up," Andy says. He spoke of what Ann loved to do, "like acting, and the things that were important in her life. She loved kids; she was our only daughter who wanted to give us grandchildren." She had talked of opening a wildlife refuge after college. "To me she had really grown up, and she was a woman," Andy says. "She was ready to go out and find her place in the world. That's the part that makes me most sad."

Kate described nursing Ann. She told of how Ann had a "lazy eye" and wore a patch as a little girl. "We worked for her to have good vision so she could drive and do all these things when she grew up. It's another thing that's lost with her death: You worked so hard to send her off into the world — what was the purpose of that now?"

"She did not spare [Conor] in any way the cost of what he did," Baliga remembers. "There were no kid gloves, none. It was really, really tough. Way tougher than anything a judge could say."

"It was excruciating to listen to them talk," Campbell says. "To look at the photo there. I still see her. It was as traumatic as anything I've ever listened to in my life."

Conor was no less affected. "Hearing the pain in their voices and what my actions had done really opened my eyes to what I've caused," Conor told me later. "Then they were like, 'All right, Conor, it's on you.' And I had to give an account of what I did." He leaned forward, placed his elbows on his knees and looked directly at the Grosmaires, who were seated opposite him. It was difficult to get started, but once he did the story came out of him in one long flow.

Ann and Conor fought on Friday night. Conor was tired and had homework and things to do the next day, so he wanted to drive home and turn in early. This was a frequent point of contention: Ann being "more of a night person," he told me later, "was sort of an ongoing issue." He promised to return to Ann's house to make breakfast, but when he overslept the next day, the fight continued. They fought by phone and text and tried to make up with a picnic that evening. Ann was excited about a good grade she got in a class and brought Champagne glasses and San Pellegrino Limonata to celebrate. But Conor forgot about the grade, and he recalled at the conference how disappointed Ann was. "It just all fell apart from there," he told me.

After sunset, they went back to his parents' house, but Conor fell asleep in the middle of a conversation. "Sunday morning rolls around, and I wake up, and she's already awake and just pissed at me," he recalled. "The fight picked up from where it left off. At some point" — this must have been hours later — "it escalated to the point to where she got all of her stuff, walked out the door, and she was just like: 'Look, I'm done. I'm leaving.' "

Conor and Ann met in chemistry class during their sophomore year in high school, and in some ways, their relationship was still adolescent. They were in love and devoted to each other, but there was also a dependence that bordered on the obsessive. They were spending so much time together senior year that Conor was fired from his job for frequently not showing up, and his father told me of "wild swings" in their relationship. There was also constant fighting. "They were both good kids," Julie McBride says, "but they were not good together." Kate Grosmaire put it another way: "It's like the argument became the relationship."

Conor was prone to bursts of irrational rage. Ann never told her parents that he had struck her several times. Michael now feels, with searing regret, that he presented a bad example of bad-tempered behavior. "Conor learned how to be angry" is how he put it to me.

"We never talked about it, you know?" Conor told me. "We never tried to be like, 'Why do you do this and why do you do that?' Or, 'This is how I'm really feeling.' That kind of communication just wasn't there."

When Ann got up to leave that Sunday morning, Conor says it wasn't clear to him if she was leaving him or just leaving, but in any case he noticed Ann had left her water bottle, and he followed her to the driveway to give it to her. He found Ann in her car, crying. As Conor related it to me, and to Ann's parents that day, Ann said to him: "You don't love me. You don't care."

Conor leaned his head through the car window, exasperated. "What do you want from all of this?" he asked. "What do you want to happen?"

"I just want you to die," she said.

Conor went back in the house, locked the door, went to his father's closet, pulled his shotgun down from a shelf, unlocked it, went to another room where the ammunition was kept and loaded the gun. He sat down in the living room, put the gun under his chin and his finger on the trigger.

"I just felt so frustrated, helpless and angry," Conor says. "I was just so sick and tired of fighting. I wanted us to work out just because, I mean, I loved the girl. I still do. I was so torn — this was the girl that just said she wants me to die. I'm sick of the fighting. I just want to die, and yet I love her, and if I kill myself she might do something to herself."

All these thoughts were running through his head when Ann started banging on the door. Conor stood up, placed the weapon on a table and let her in. They went into his bedroom, and a few minutes later Conor went to get her something to drink. When he returned, he found her lying on the couch, breathing in a way that seemed to indicate distress. Her mysterious behavior made him so angry that he started screaming: "Let me help you! Tell me what's wrong!" Conor says that he would frequently fall into this "wrathful anger," and on this day "there was so much anger, and I kept snapping." Ann started sobbing, saying that Conor didn't care and that she wanted to die. "At this point, I just lost it," Conor says. He left the room and got the gun. Ann started to follow him, but she may have stumbled or tripped, because when Conor returned with the gun, she was on her knees half-way between the couch and the door. Conor was frustrated, exhausted and angry and "not thinking straight at all."

He pointed the gun at her, thinking, he says, that he could "scare her" so that "maybe she would snap out of it."

"Is this what you want?" he yelled. "Do you want to die?"

"No, don't!" Ann held out her hand. Conor fired.

As Conor told the story, Andy's whole body began to shake. "Let me get this right," he said, and asked Conor about Ann being on her knees. Baliga remembers Andy's demeanor at this moment: "Andy is a very gentle person, but there was a way at that moment that he was extremely strong. There was just this incredible force of the strong, protective, powerful father coursing through him." Conor answered, clarifying precisely how helpless Ann was at the moment he took her life.

The Grosmaires remember that at this point, Campbell suggested a break. Campbell told me that he understood "the process was going to be horrific" and that he was the only one present with the power to halt it. During the break, he approached the Grosmaires in the hallway.

"You all had enough?" he asked. "I'm here for you all, and I don't mind being the heavy." Kate thanked him but declined his offer to end the conference early. As Campbell backed away, Baliga approached the Grosmaires. "I thought it was going to make sense," Andy told her. Later, Andy told me that he had fantasized or hoped that maybe it had been an accident, maybe Conor's finger had slipped — that he would hear something unexpected to help him make sense of his daughter's death. But Conor's recitation didn't bring that kind of solace.

When the group returned to the circle, Conor continued. He didn't try to shirk responsibility at the conference or in long conversations with me about the murder. "What I did was inexcusable," he told me. "There is no why, there are no excuses, there is no reason." He told Ann's parents that he had no plans to shoot their daughter. Still, he said, "on some subconscious level, I guess, I wanted it all to end. I don't know what happened. I just — emotions were overwhelming." He said he didn't remember deciding to pull the trigger, but he recognizes that it wasn't an accident, either.

Conor said he stood there, ears ringing, with the smell of gunpowder in the air. The thought came into his head that he ought to kill himself, but he couldn't muster the will. Instead, he left the house and drove around in a daze until he decided to turn himself in.

Julie McBride was devastated. "I was sitting right next to him. It was awful to hear and to know: This is my son telling this. This is my son who did this."

When it was Michael McBride's turn to speak, sorrow overtook him and he told the group that if he had ever thought his shotgun would have harmed another person, he never would have kept it. Kate Grosmaire didn't bring it up at the conference, but she says she has thought a lot about that gun. "If that gun had not been in the house, our daughter would be alive," she told me.

When everyone had spoken, Baliga turned to the Grosmaires, and acknowledging their immediate loss, she asked what they would like to see happen to attempt restitution. Kate looked at Conor and with great emotion told him that he would need "to do the good works of two people because Ann is not here to do hers."

The punitive element came last. Before the conference, Kate, who doesn't put much stock in the rehabilitative possibilities of prison, told Baliga that she would suggest a five-year sentence. Listening to Conor, however, she began to feel different, and when she was called on to speak, she said he should receive no less than 5 years, no more than 15.

Andy Grosmaire, sitting beside his wife, went next. He was so deeply affected by what he had heard, it was all he could do to say, "10 to 15 years." The McBrides concurred. Conor said he didn't think he should have a say.

All eyes turned to Campbell. A restorative-justice circle is supposed to conclude with a consensus decision, but Campbell refused to suggest a punishment. He only said he heard what was discussed and would take it under consideration. "I think the ultimate decision on punishment should be made based on cool reflection of the facts and the evidence in the case," Campbell told me later. "I don't think those conferences are the best prism for that."

The Grosmaires were deeply disappointed. Andy in particular imagined that the end of the conference circle would be the beginning of the young man's redemption. They expected a plea bargain would be struck, and they could go on. Instead they had no idea where Campbell stood. "Had the circle really worked?" Kate asked.

Campbell would consult with community leaders, the head of a local domestic-violence shelter and others before arriving at the sentence he would offer McBride. He told me that his boss, Willie Meggs, the state attorney, who Campbell once believed would never sign off on a sentence of less than 40 years for Conor, was "extremely supportive" once he understood the Grosmaires' perspective. "He wanted to be sure I had gone through the proper analysis," Campbell says, "and that it was for the right motivations. Because he knew there would be a backlash."

Three weeks after the conference, citing Conor's "senseless act of domestic violence," Campbell wrote the Grosmaires to inform them he would offer Conor a choice: a 20-year sentence plus 10 years of probation, or 25 years in prison. Conor took the 20 years, plus probation.

Campbell told me that in arriving at those numbers, he needed to feel certain that "a year or 20 years down the road, I could tell somebody why I did it. Because if Conor gets out in 20 years and goes and kills his next girlfriend, I've screwed up terrible. So I hope I'm right."

IN MARCH THE Grosmaires invited me to their home, on Tallahassee's northern fringe. We sat down in their living room, near a modest shrine to Ann: items that represented her at the conference are there, along with her cellphone and a small statue of an angel that Kate splurged for not long after Ann's death that reminds her of Ann.

The Grosmaires said they didn't forgive Conor for his sake but for their own. "Everything I feel, I can feel because we forgave Conor," Kate said. "Because we could forgive, people can say her name. People can think about my daughter, and they don't have to think, Oh, the murdered girl. I think that when people can't forgive, they're stuck. All they can feel is the emotion surrounding that moment. I can be sad, but I don't have to stay stuck in that moment where this awful thing happened. Because if I do, I may never come out of it. Forgiveness for me was self-preservation."

Still, their forgiveness affected Conor, too, and not only in the obvious way of reducing his sentence. "With the Grosmaires' forgiveness," he told me, "I could accept the responsibility and not be condemned." Forgiveness doesn't make him any less guilty, and it doesn't absolve him of what he did, but in refusing to become Conor's enemy, the Grosmaires deprived him of a certain kind of refuge — of feeling abandoned and hated — and placed the reckoning for the crime squarely in his hands. I spoke to Conor for six hours over three days, in a prison administrator's office at the Liberty Correctional Institution near Tallahassee. At one point he sat with his hands and fingers open in front of him, as if he were holding something. Eyes cast downward, he said, "There are moments when you realize: I am in prison. I am in prison because I killed someone. I am in prison because I killed the girl I loved."

Conor got a job at the prison's law library. He spends a lot of his time reading novels by George R. R. Martin, the author of the "Game of Thrones" series. He enrolled voluntarily in the anger-management class offered at the prison and continues to meet with his classmates since completing it. He told me that when he gets out he plans to volunteer in animal shelters, because Ann loved animals. As a condition of his probation, Conor will be required to speak to local groups about teen-dating violence. His parents visit him regularly, and they talk on the phone almost every day. They talk about his sister, Katy, baseball and food, Michael says, as well as the issues he needs to focus on to come out a better person than he was when he went in. "As long as I'm self-motivated enough," Conor says, "I can really improve myself." The Grosmaires come, too, about once a month.

"I'm not worried about him getting out in 20 years at all," Baliga told me. "We got to look more deeply at the root of where this behavior came from than we would have had it gone a trial route — the anger issues in the family, exploring the drama in their relationship, the whole conglomeration of factors that led to that moment. There's no explaining what happened, but there was just a much more nuanced conversation about it, which can give everyone more confidence that Conor will never do this again. And the Grosmaires got answers to questions that would have been difficult to impossible to get in a trial."

Not everyone felt comfortable with the restorative-justice circle or how it resolved: there were angry letters on local news sites denouncing the sentence as too light. Ann's sisters supported their parents' decision to forgive Conor and seek restorative justice but declined to participate in the process (they also declined to speak to me). In hindsight, Kate sees the restorative-justice process as a sort of end in itself. "Just being able to have the circle made it a success," Kate said.

Andy felt a little differently. "Hearing Conor," he said, "I made sounds I've never heard myself make. To hear that your daughter was on the floor saying 'no' and holding her hands up and still be shot is just — it's just not. ..." He tried to explain the horror of such knowledge, but it's not easy. Even experiencing the deaths of other family members, he said, has given him "no context" to understand what happened to Ann. Andy doesn't attribute Ann's death to "God's plan" and rolls his eyes at "God just wanted another angel" sentimentality. But not being "stuck" in anger seems to give the Grosmaires the emotional distance necessary to grapple with such questions without the gravity of their grief pulling them into a black hole. I talked a lot to Kate and Andy over several months. They don't intellectualize what happened or repress emotions — I saw them cry and I heard them laugh — but they were always able to speak thoughtfully about Ann's death and its aftermath.

As much as the Grosmaires say that forgiveness helped them, so, too, has the story of their forgiveness. They've spoken about it to church groups and prayer breakfasts around Tallahassee and plan to do more talks. The story is a signpost in the wilderness, something solid and decent they can return to while wandering in this parallel universe without their youngest daughter.

Kate Grosmaire keeps asking herself if she has really forgiven Conor. "I think about it all the time," she said. "Is that forgiveness still there? Have I released that debt?" Even as the answer comes back yes, she says, it can't erase her awareness of what she no longer has. "Forgiving Conor doesn't change the fact that Ann is not with us. My daughter was shot, and she died. I walk by her empty bedroom at least twice a day."

PAUL TULLIS is a freelance writer. His last article for the magazine was about a controversial treatment for multiple sclerosis.

Opening Up, Students Transform a Vicious Circle

BY PATRICIA LEIGH BROWN | APRIL 3, 2013

OAKLAND, CALIF. — There is little down time in Eric Butler's classroom.

"My daddy got arrested this morning," Mercedes Morgan, a distraught senior, told the students gathered there.

Mr. Butler's mission is to help defuse grenades of conflict at Ralph J. Bunche High School, the end of the line for students with a history of getting into trouble. He is the school's coordinator for restorative justice, a program increasingly offered in schools seeking an alternative to "zero tolerance" policies like suspension and expulsion.

The approach now taking root in 21 Oakland schools, and in Chicago, Denver and Portland, Ore., tries to nip problems and violence in the bud by forging closer, franker relationships among students, teachers and administrators. It encourages young people to come up with meaningful reparations for their wrongdoing while challenging them to develop empathy for one another through "talking circles" led by facilitators like Mr. Butler.

Even before her father's arrest on a charge of shooting at a car, Mercedes was prone to anger. "When I get angry, I blank out," she said. She listed some reasons on a white board — the names of friends and classmates who lost their lives to Oakland's escalating violence. Among them was Kiante Campbell, a senior shot and killed during a downtown arts festival in February. His photocopied image was plastered around Mr. Butler's room, along with white roses left from a restorative "grief circle."

Restorative justice adopts some techniques of the circle practice that is a way of life for indigenous cultures, fostering collaboration. Students speak without interruption, for example, to show mutual respect.

Mr. Butler with a student at Ralph J. Bunche High School in Oakland.

"A lot of these young people don't have adults to cry to," said Be-Naiah Williams, an after-school coordinator at Bunche whose 21-year-old brother was gunned down two years ago in a nightclub. "So whatever emotion they feel, they go do."

Oakland expanded the program after an initial success six years ago. Since then, the need for an alternative discipline has become more urgent: Last year, the district faced a Department of Education civil rights investigation into high suspension and expulsion rates, particularly among African-American boys.

A report by the Urban Strategies Council, a research and policy organization in Oakland, showed that African-American boys made up 17 percent of the district's enrollment but 42 percent of all suspensions, and were six times more likely to be suspended than their white male classmates. Many disciplinary actions were for "defiance" — nonviolent infractions like texting in class or using profanity with a teacher.

A body of research indicates that lost class time due to suspension and expulsion results in alienation and often early involvement with the juvenile justice system, said Nancy Riestenberg, of the Minnesota Department of Education, an early adopter of restorative justice. Being on "high alert" for violence is not conducive to learning, she added.

Many studies have concluded that zero-tolerance policies do not make schools safer.

"We're a terribly violent community," said Junious Williams, the chief executive of the Urban Strategies Council. "We have not done very much around teaching kids alternatives to conflict that escalates into violence."

Among the lost youngsters was Damon Smith, now an A student at Bunche, who said he had been suspended more than 15 times. "You start thinking it's cool," he said. "You think you're going to come back to school and catch up, but unless you're a genius you won't. It made me want to mess up even more."

Damon, 18, said restorative justice sessions helped him view his behavior through a different lens. "I didn't know how to express emotions with my mouth. I knew how to hit people," he said. "I feel I can go to someone now."

Eight of Oakland's participating schools have full-time coordinators like Mr. Butler, whose work is financed by the nonprofit Restorative Justice for Oakland Youth. He is often called on to handle delicate situations: 90 percent of the 250 students at Bunche have had run-ins with the juvenile system or lived in foster homes.

In one circle, students discussed racism. In another, a girl confided that she had been molested as a child. "Those boys who looked scary wrapped their arms around this girl," Mr. Butler said. "That's what's missing for our kids. It's harder to fight people you feel a closeness to."

Recently, it appeared that jealousy had triggered a fight between two classmates. Ebony Monroe, a new student, was wearing short shorts. Jameelah Garry, who recently had a baby, was wearing a baggy flannel shirt. Jameelah slugged her. "I don't like her," she explained.

"If your kid was in this situation, what advice would you give her?" Mr. Butler asked gently.

Jameelah went silent, then said, "I got an anger problem, I'll be honest with you." She started to cry, tears welling up on glue-on eyelashes. "I lost my brother last year," she said. "Charles. He was shot in the head after an altercation in East Oakland."

She took off a sleeve to reveal a teal tattoo in his memory. No one at the school had known.

Betsye Steele, the principal, said that without the circle, and the trust it developed, the major source of Jameelah's bad behavior would not have been discovered and might have escalated.

Since the program started, the school reduced its overall suspension rate to 8 percent in 2012 from 12 percent in 2011.

But restorative justice is not a quick fix, teachers' union officials and legal experts warn. "You're changing a culture that has been in place for a long time," said Mary Louise Frampton, an adjunct law professor at the University of California, Berkeley. "It's a multiyear process."

It is also not a treatment for mental illness or ideal for situations with major power imbalances, like bullying, said Barbara McClung, the district's coordinator for behavior health initiatives. "Not every student will acknowledge they caused harm," she added.

Approaches to restorative justice vary nationwide. Some districts allow suspensions and expulsions but now require stricter justification. Others, under pressure to reduce suspensions, put students on "administrative leave" instead. Some schools focus on formal mediation and reparation while others, like Bunche, are more spontaneous.

A recent circle at Bunche for Jeffrey, who was on the verge of expulsion for habitual vandalism, included an Oakland police officer, and the conversation turned to the probability that Jeffrey would wind up incarcerated or on the streets. The student had told Mr. Butler that he was being pressured to join a gang.

"Cat, you got five people right now invested in your well-being," Mr. Butler told him. "This is a matter of life or death." Jeffrey agreed to

The circle practice has been a way of life for indigenous cultures, a way of fostering collaboration. Restorative justice adopts the techniques of letting students speak without interruption, to show respect. Students, staff and faculty members talked through an issue during a "talking circle."

go to Mr. Butler's classroom every day at third period to do his schoolwork.

Mr. Butler, who grew up in a vast segregated housing project in New Orleans, knows the urge for retribution: Two years ago, his sister was murdered by her boyfriend. "I wanted my quart of blood," he told students disturbed by Kiante Campbell's death.

Then the boyfriend's mother showed up, seeking forgiveness. "This brave little woman knocked on the door in her robe and flip-flops," he told his classroom. "The want for revenge in my stomach lifted."

Keeping students in school, focused on the future, is at the core of his work. So every Friday afternoon he tells them: "Y'all gotta come back Monday. Come back. I gotta see you."

"We're all we've got," he said. "And we need to start thinking that way."

By Talking, Inmates and Victims Make Things 'More Right'

BY DINA KRAFT | JULY 5, 2014

NORFOLK, MASS. — For many of his 15 years behind the soaring prison walls here, Muhammad Sahin managed to suppress thinking of his victims' anguish — even that of the one who haunted him most, a toddler who peeked out from beneath her blankets the night he shot and killed her mother in a gang-ordered hit.

But he found it impossible to stop the tears as he sat in a circle together with Deborah Wornum, a woman whose son was murdered, and more than a dozen other men serving terms for homicide and other violent crimes. Each participant — victim and inmate — had a very different, personal story to share with the encounter groups that met here on a recent weekend in a process called restorative justice.

Ms. Wornum, 58, talked about the summer night three years ago when her son Aaron, a 25-year-old musician, walked out of their home with a cheerful "Be right back." Forty minutes later the phone rang. It was a hospital; her son had been shot. He took his final breath in her arms.

"You touched me the most because it really made me understand what I put the family through," said Mr. Sahin, 37, who was 22 when he killed the young mother. Taking a deep breath, broad shoulders bent forward, he continued. "I really don't know how to overcome this or if I can overcome it. I've done a lot of bad stuff in my life. But I've reached a place where I'm not numb anymore."

Lifting his head to look directly at Ms. Wornum, he projected his crime onto the murder of her son: "I kind of feel like I caused the pain, like I'm the one who committed the crime."

The unusual two-day gathering took place south of Boston at the Massachusetts Correctional Institution at Norfolk, one of the state's oldest prisons as well as its largest, with about 1,500 inmates. Under

Inmates applauded Janet Connors after she told the story of her son's murder at the Restorative Justice Retreat at the state prison in Norfolk, Mass., last month.

the whirring of overhead fans in an auditorium of exposed red brick, it brought 150 inmates together with victims, judges, prosecutors and mediators. Gov. Deval Patrick attended briefly and met with a small group of those present.

Restorative justice, a process with roots in Native American and other indigenous cultures that resurfaced in the United States and abroad in the 1970s, has begun to make headway in some states, including Massachusetts, where legislation was introduced last year to promote its practice. It brings offenders and victims together voluntarily. Offenders take responsibility and acknowledge the impact their actions had on their victims and loved ones as well as their own families and neighborhoods. The victim is given a chance to ask questions of the offenders and share how their lives were affected by the crime. Advocates say it is key to rehabilitation and reduced recidivism.

"It tries to make things not right — but at least more right," said Karen Lischinsky, a sociologist and volunteer coordinator of the prison's restorative-justice group, which helped facilitate the gathering. "Nothing will bring back those killed."

In September, Massachusetts will pilot a curriculum on restorative justice, modeled on a program called the Victim Offender Education Group, which was developed for California's San Quentin State Prison. Meeting weekly for 34 weeks, participants will undergo a probing process aimed at acquiring accountability for the harm they caused.

Advocates for restorative justice say the concept is often misunderstood as being "soft" on crime. But in a prison setting that does not usually challenge offenders to take personal responsibility — and where some even convince themselves they did nothing wrong — the approach offers a marked contrast. In interviews with the incarcerated men and in the dialogue circles, a common theme was how their focus when they entered prison was on survival, not reflecting on the actions that had brought them here.

Norfolk's restorative-justice group formed three years ago. After some tension among inmates in 2010, several "lifers" asked for assistance in forming the group in the hope of promoting a peaceful prison culture.

At the retreat, members of the group greeted visitors, introduced speakers, took part in public apologies and helped facilitate the circles. They spoke of signs of transformation inside the prison. Where four years ago no one knew what restorative justice was, now it is heard in conversations in the cellblocks and in the yard. Participants spoke of the importance of getting their message to reverberate, too, in their home neighborhoods, many of which are marred by violence and drugs.

One participant was David Myland. Facilitating a circle on forgiveness, the ruddy-faced 31-year-old from the Cape Cod area, with a stopwatch around his neck and a pen tucked behind an ear, could at first pass as a swim coach. He is serving time for second-degree murder during a home invasion when he was 20.

"I did some rotten things in prison and I've done some rotten things in the community, but the only reason I can do what I do now is because brothers and sisters have given me the opportunity to learn from them and go through a process where I can gain the insight I need to heal me. So I can go on and help others," Mr. Myland said.

Janet Connors, 64, a longtime community activist, was the first in Massachusetts to undergo a mediated dialogue, with two of the young men responsible for her son Joel's stabbing death.

Speaking in a loud, firm voice, she looked out at her audience and told the prisoners that calling them monsters was a disservice to everyone: "Holding you in your humanity — it's how we hold each other accountable."

"We're willing to risk a lot to open up the lines of communication," she said. "To really figure out what to do to stop the nonsense — nonsense is too weak a word. To stop this horror that is taking people's lives."

"I want you all to be part of the story," she added. "We as survivors have to be included because there is no restorative justice without us."

During a break for lunch, Ms. Connors checked in on Ms. Wornum.

"It was rough," Ms. Wornum told her.

Ms. Connors smiled and confided: "Sometimes I say Joel is with me on this ride. Or I say, no, he is looking down on me saying, 'What are you doing?' Sometimes you just go back and forth."

One inmate, who asked not to be identified to protect the privacy of his victims' families, said of the interaction: "There's a different level of connection — guys open up in the group, and you realize that deep down inside men are the same. And when you start to see that you understand yourself better."

Asked what he would tell the teenager he was when he committed his crime, he said, choking up: "I'd probably just hug him. That's it."

The Radical Humaneness of Norway's Halden Prison

BY JESSICA BENKO | MARCH 26, 2015

The goal of the Norwegian penal system is to get inmates out of it.

LIKE EVERYTHING ELSE in Norway, the two-hour drive southeast from Oslo seemed impossibly civilized. The highways were perfectly maintained and painted, the signs clear and informative and the speed-monitoring cameras primly intolerant. My destination was the town of Halden, which is on the border with Sweden, straddling a narrow fjord guarded by a 17th-century fortress. I drove down winding roads flanked in midsummer by rich green fields of young barley and dense yellow carpets of rapeseed plants in full flower. Cows clustered in wood-fenced pastures next to neat farmsteads in shades of rust and ocher. On the outskirts of town, across from a road parting dark pine forest, the turnoff to Norway's newest prison was marked by a modest sign that read, simply, HALDEN FENGSEL. There were no signs warning against picking up hitchhikers, no visible fences. Only the 25-foot-tall floodlights rising along the edges hinted that something other than grazing cows lay ahead.

Smooth, featureless concrete rose on the horizon like the wall of a dam as I approached; nearly four times as tall as a man, it snaked along the crests of the hills, its top curled toward me as if under pressure. This was the outer wall of Halden Fengsel, which is often called the world's most humane maximum-security prison. I walked up the quiet driveway to the entrance and presented myself to a camera at the main door. There were no coils of razor wire in sight, no lethal electric fences, no towers manned by snipers — nothing violent, threatening or dangerous. And yet no prisoner has ever tried to escape. I rang the intercom, the lock disengaged with a click and I stepped inside.

To anyone familiar with the American correctional system, Halden seems alien. Its modern, cheerful and well-appointed facilities, the relative freedom of movement it offers, its quiet and peaceful atmosphere — these qualities are so out of sync with the forms of imprisonment found in the United States that you could be forgiven for doubting whether Halden is a prison at all. It is, of course, but it is also something more: the physical expression of an entire national philosophy about the relative merits of punishment and forgiveness.

The treatment of inmates at Halden is wholly focused on helping to prepare them for a life after they get out. Not only is there no death penalty in Norway; there are no life sentences. The maximum sentence for most crimes is 21 years — even for Anders Behring Breivik, who is responsible for probably the deadliest recorded rampage in the world, in which he killed 77 people and injured hundreds more in 2011 by detonating a bomb at a government building in Oslo and then opening fire at a nearby summer camp. Because Breivik was sentenced to "preventive detention," however, his term can be extended indefinitely for five years at a time, if he is deemed a continuing threat to society by the court. "Better out than in" is an unofficial motto of the Norwegian Correctional Service, which makes a reintegration guarantee to all released inmates. It works with other government agencies to secure a home, a job and access to a supportive social network for each inmate before release; Norway's social safety net also provides health care, education and a pension to all citizens. With one of the highest per capita gross domestic products of any country in the world, thanks to the profits from oil production in the North Sea, Norway is in a good position to provide all of this, and spending on the Halden prison runs to more than $93,000 per inmate per year, compared with just $31,000 for prisoners in the United States, according to the Vera Institute of Justice, a nonprofit research and advocacy organization.

That might sound expensive. But if the United States incarcerated its citizens at the same low rate as the Norwegians do (75 per 100,000 residents, versus roughly 700), it could spend that much per inmate and still save more than $45 billion a year. At a time when the American correctional system is under scrutiny — over the harshness of its sentences, its overreliance on solitary confinement, its racial disparities — citizens might ask themselves what all that money is getting them, besides 2.2 million incarcerated people and the hardships that fall on the families they leave behind. The extravagant brutality of the American approach to prisons is not working, and so it might just be worth looking for lessons at the opposite extreme, here in a sea of *blabaerskog*, or blueberry forest.

"THIS PUNISHMENT, TAKING away their freedom — the sign of that is the wall, of course," Gudrun Molden, one of the Halden prison's architects, said on a drizzly morning a few days after I arrived. As we stood on a ridge, along with Jan Stromnes, the assistant warden, it was silent but for the chirping of birds and insects and a hoarse fluttering of birch leaves disturbed by the breeze. The prison is secluded from the surrounding farmland by the blueberry woods, which are the native forest of southeastern Norway: blue-black spruce, slender Scotch pine with red-tinged trunks and silver-skinned birches over a dense understory of blueberry bushes, ferns and mosses in deep shade. It is an ecosystem that evokes deep nostalgia in Norway, where picking wild berries is a near-universal summer pastime for families, and where the right to do so on uncultivated land is protected by law.

Norway banned capital punishment for civilians in 1902, and life sentences were abolished in 1981. But Norwegian prisons operated much like their American counterparts until 1998. That was the year Norway's Ministry of Justice reassessed the Correctional Service's goals and methods, putting the explicit focus on rehabilitating prisoners through education, job training and therapy. A second wave of change in 2007 made a priority of reintegration, with a special emphasis on helping inmates find housing and work with a steady income before they are even released. Halden was the first prison built after this overhaul, and so rehabilitation became the underpinning of its design process. Every aspect of the facility was designed to ease psychological pressures, mitigate conflict and minimize interpersonal friction. Hence the blueberry forest.

"Nature is a rehabilitation thing now," Molden said. Researchers are working to quantify the benefits of sunlight and fresh air in treating depression. But Molden viewed nature's importance for Norwegian inmates as far more personal. "We don't think of it as a rehabilitation," she said. "We think of it as a basic element in our growing up." She gestured to the knoll we stood on and the 12 acres of *blabaerskog* preserved on the prison grounds, echoing the canopy visible on the far side. Even elsewhere in Europe, most high-security prison plots are scraped completely flat and denuded of vegetation as security measures. "A lot of the staff when we started out came from other prisons in Norway," Stromnes said. "They were a little bit astonished by the trees and the number of them. Shouldn't they be taken away? And what if they climb up, the inmates? As we said, Well, if they climb up, then they can sit there until they get tired, and then they will come down." He laughed. "Never has anyone tried to hide inside. But if they should run in there, they won't get very far — they're still inside."

"Inside" meant inside the wall. The prison's defining feature, the wall is visible everywhere the inmates go, functioning as an inescapable reminder of their imprisonment. Because the prison buildings were purposely built to a human scale, with none more than two stories in height and all modest in breadth, the wall becomes an outsize presence; it looms everywhere, framed by the cell windows, shadowing the exercise yards, its pale horizontal spread emphasized by the dark vertical lines of the trees. The two primary responsibilities of the Correctional Service — detention and rehabilitation — are in perpetual tension with each other, and the architects felt that single wall could represent both. "We trusted the wall," Molden said, to serve as a symbol and an instrument of punishment.

When Molden and her collaborators visited the site in 2002, in preparing for the international competition to design the prison, they spent every minute they were allowed walking around it, trying to absorb the *genius loci*, the spirit of the place. They felt they should use as much of the site as possible, requiring inmates to walk outside to their daily commitments of school or work or therapy, over uneven ground, up and down hills, traveling to and from home, as they would in the world outside. They wound up arranging the prison's living quarters in a ring, which we could now see sloping down the hill on either side of us. In the choice of materials, the architects were inspired by the sober palette of the trees, mosses and bedrock all around; the primary building element is kiln-fired brick, blackened with some of the original red showing through. The architects used silvery galvanized-steel panels as a "hard" material to represent detention, and untreated larch wood, a low-maintenance species that weathers from taupe to soft gray, as a "soft" material associated with rehabilitation and growth.

The Correctional Service emphasizes what it calls "dynamic security," a philosophy that sees interpersonal relationships between the staff and the inmates as the primary factor in maintaining safety within the prison. They contrast this with the approach dominant in high-security prisons elsewhere in the world, which they call "static security." Static security relies on an environment designed to prevent an inmate with bad intentions from carrying them out. Inmates at those prisons are watched at a remove through cameras, contained by remote-controlled doors, prevented from vandalism or weapon-making by tamper-proof furniture, encumbered by shackles or officer escorts when moved. Corrections officers there are trained to control prisoners with as little interaction as possible, minimizing the risk of altercation.

Dynamic security focuses on preventing bad intentions from developing in the first place. Halden's officers are put in close quarters with the inmates as often as possible; the architects were instructed to make the guard stations tiny and cramped, to encourage officers to spend time in common rooms with the inmates instead. The guards socialize with the inmates every day, in casual conversation, often over tea or coffee or meals. Inmates can be monitored via surveillance cameras on the prison grounds, but they often move unaccompanied by guards, requiring a modest level of trust, which the administrators believe is crucial to their progress. Nor are there surveillance cameras in the classrooms or most of the workshops, or in the common rooms, the cell hallways or the cells themselves. The inmates have the opportunity to act out, but somehow they choose not to. In five years, the isolation cell furnished with a limb-restraining bed has never been used.

IT IS TEMPTING to chalk up all this reasonableness to something peculiar in Norwegian socialization, some sort of civility driven core-deep into the inmates since birth, or perhaps attribute it to their racial and ethnic homogeneity as a group. But in actuality, only around three-fifths of the inmates are legal Norwegian citizens. The rest have come from more than 30 other countries (mostly in Eastern Europe, Africa and the Middle East) and speak little or no Norwegian; English is the lingua franca, a necessity for the officers to communicate with foreign prisoners.

Of the 251 inmates, nearly half are imprisoned for violent crimes like murder, assault or rape; a third are in for smuggling or selling drugs. Nevertheless, violent incidents and even threats are rare, and nearly all take place in Unit A. It is the prison's most restrictive unit, housing inmates who require close psychiatric or medical supervision or who committed crimes that would make them unpopular in Units B and C, the prison's more open "living" cell blocks, where the larger population of inmates mixes during the day for work, schooling and therapy programs.

I met some of the prisoners of Unit A one afternoon in the common room of an eight-man cell block. I was asked to respect the inmates' preferences for anonymity or naming, and for their choices in discussing their cases with me. The Norwegian news media does not often identify suspects or convicts by name, so confirming the details of their stories was not always possible. I sat on an orange vinyl couch next to a wooden shelving unit with a few haphazard piles of board games and magazines and legal books. On the other side of the room, near a window overlooking the unit's gravel yard, a couple of inmates were absorbed in a card game with a guard.

An inmate named Omar passed me a freshly pressed heart-shaped waffle over my shoulder on a paper plate, interrupting an intense monologue directed at me in excellent English by Chris Giske, a large man with a thick goatee and a shaved head who was wearing a heavy gold chain over a T-shirt that strained around his barrel-shaped torso.

"You have heard about the case? Sigrid?" Giske asked me. "It's one of the biggest cases in Norway."

In 2012, a 16-year-old girl named Sigrid Schjetne vanished while walking home one night, and her disappearance gripped the country. Her body was found a month later, and Giske's conviction in the case made him one of the most reviled killers in Norwegian history.

He explained to me that he asked to transfer out of Unit A, but that officials declined to move him. "They don't want me in prison," he said. "They want me in the psychiatric thing. I don't know why."

He was denied the transfer, I was later told, partly because of a desire not to outrage the other inmates, and partly because of significant concern over his mental health — and his history of unprovoked extreme violence against young women unfortunate enough to cross his path. Giske had previously spent two years in prison after attacking a woman with a crowbar. This time, there was disagreement among doctors over whether he belonged in a hospital or in prison. Until the question was settled, he was the responsibility of the staff at Halden. It was not the first, second or even third casual meal I had shared with a man convicted of murder since I arrived at the beginning of the week, but it was the first time I felt myself recoil on instinct. (After my visit, Giske was transferred to a psychiatric institution.)

Omar handed me a vacuum-sealed slice of what appeared to be flexible plastic, its wrapper decorated with a drawing of cheerful red dairy barns.

"It's fantastic!" he exclaimed. "When you are in Norway, you must try this! The first thing I learned, it was this. Brown cheese."

According to the packaging, brown cheese is one of the things that "make Norwegians Norwegians," a calorie-dense fuel of fat and sugar salvaged from whey discarded during the cheese-making process, which is cooked down for half a day until all that remains are caramelized milk sugars in a thick, sticky residue. With enthusiastic encouragement from the inmates, I peeled open the packaging and placed the glossy square on my limp waffle, following their instructions to fold the waffle as you would a taco, or a New York slice. To their great amusement, I winced as I tried to swallow what tasted to me like a paste of spray cheese mixed with fudge.

Another guard walked in and sat down next to me on the couch. "It's allowed to say you don't like it," she said.

Are Hoidal, the prison's warden, laughed from the doorway behind us and accepted his third waffle of the day. He had explained to me earlier, in response to my raised eyebrows, that in keeping with the prison's commitment to "normalcy," even the inmates in this block gather once a week to partake of waffles, which are a weekly ritual in most Norwegian homes.

At Halden, some inmates train for cooking certificates in the prison's professional-grade kitchen classroom, where I was treated to chocolate mousse presented in a wineglass, a delicate nest of orange zest curled on top. But most of the kitchen activity is more ordinary. I never entered a cell block without receiving offers of tea or coffee, an essential element of even the most basic Norwegian hospitality, and was always earnestly invited to share meals. The best meal I had in Norway — spicy lasagna, garlic bread and a salad with sun-dried tomatoes — was made by an inmate who had spent almost half of his 40 years in prison. "Every time, you make an improvement," he said of his cooking skills.

WHEN I FIRST met the inmates of C8, a special unit focused on addiction recovery, they were returning to their block laden with green nylon reusable bags filled with purchases from their weekly visit to the prison grocery shop, which is well stocked, carrying snacks and nonperishables but also a colorful assortment of produce, dairy products and meat. The men piled bags of food for communal suppers on the kitchen island on one side of their common room and headed back to their cells with personal items — fruit, soda, snacks, salami — to stash in their minifridges.

I met Tom, an inmate in his late 40s, as he was unpacking groceries on the counter: eggs, bacon, bread, cream, onions, tomato sauce, ground beef, lettuce, almonds, olives, frozen shrimp. Tom had a hoarse voice and a graying blond goatee, and his sleeveless basketball jersey exposed an assortment of tattoos decorating thick arms. His head was shaved smooth, with "F___ the Police" inked in cursive along the right side of his skull; the left side said "RESPECT" in inch-tall letters. A small block of text under his right eye was blacked out, and under his left eye was "666." A long seam ran up the back of his neck and scalp, a remnant of a high-speed motorcycle accident that left him in a coma the last time he was out of prison.

"You are alone now, yeah?" Tom nodded toward the room behind me. I turned around to look.

There were maybe eight inmates around — playing a soccer video game on the modular couch, folding laundry dried on a rack in the corner by large windows overlooking the exercise yard, dealing cards at the dining table — but no guards. Tom searched my face for signs of alarm. The convictions represented among this group included murder, weapons possession and assault.

I was a little surprised, but I stayed nonchalant. I might have expected a bit more supervision — perhaps a quick briefing on safety protocol and security guidelines — but the guards could see us through the long windows of their station, sandwiched between the common rooms of C7 and C8. It was the first of many times I would be left alone with inmates in a common room or in a cell at the end of a hallway, the staff retreating to make space for candid conversation. "It's O.K.," Tom assured me, with what I thought sounded like a hint of pride.

A man named Yassin, the uncontested pastry king of C8, politely motioned for me to move aside so he could get to the baking pans in the cabinet at my feet. When Halden opened, there was a wave of foreign news reports containing snarky, florid descriptions of the "posh," "luxurious" prison, comparing its furnishings to those of a "boutique hotel." In reality, the furniture is not dissimilar from what you might find in an American college dorm. The truly striking difference is that it is *normal* furniture, not specially designed to prevent it from being turned into shivs, arson fuel or other instruments of violence. The kitchen also provides ample weapons if a prisoner were so inclined. As one inmate pointed out to me, the cabinets on the wall contained ceramic plates and glass cups, the drawers held metal silverware and there were a couple of large kitchen knives tethered by lengths of rubber-coated wire.

"If you want to ask me something, come on, no problem," Tom said, throwing open his hands in invitation. "I'm not very good in English."

Yassin stood up, laughing. "You speak very nice, Tom! It is prison English!" Yassin speaks Arabic and English and is also fluent in Norwegian, a requirement for living in the drug-treatment block, where group and individual counseling is conducted in Norwegian. Like many in the prison, Tom never finished high school. He was raised in a boys' home and has been in and out of prison, where English is common, for more than 30 years. (Yassin's first prison sentence began at 15. Now 29 and close to finishing his sentence for selling drugs, he wants to make a change and thinks he might like to run a scared-straight-style program for teenagers. Before this most recent arrest, the background photo on his Facebook profile was the Facebook logo recreated in white powder on a blue background, with a straw coming in for the snort. He immigrated to Norway as a child with his Moroccan family by way of Dubai.)

"I don't leave Norway," Tom said. "I love my country." He extended his arm with his fist clenched, showing a forearm covered in a "NORGE" tattoo shaded in the colors of the Norwegian flag. But I couldn't detect any tension between Tom and Yassin in the kitchen. Tom was adamant that overcoming his substance-abuse problem was his responsibility alone. But he conceded that the environment at Halden, and the availability of therapists, made it easier. Compared with other prisons, "it's quiet," he said. "No fighting, no drugs, no problem," he added. "You're safe."

The officers try to head off any tensions that could lead to violence. If inmates are having problems with one another, an officer or prison chaplain brings them together for a mediation session that continues until they have agreed to maintain peace and have shaken hands. Even members of rival gangs agree not to fight inside, though the promise doesn't extend to after their release. The few incidents of violence at Halden have been almost exclusively in Unit A, among the inmates with more serious psychiatric illnesses.

If an inmate does violate the rules, the consequences are swift, consistent and evenly applied. Repeated misbehavior or rule violations can result in cell confinement during regular work hours, sometimes without TV. One inmate claimed that an intrepid prisoner from Eastern Europe somehow managed to hack his TV to connect to the Internet and had it taken away for five months. ("Five months!" the inmate marveled to me. "I don't understand how he survived.")

IT IS PERHAPS hard to believe that Halden, or Norway more broadly, could hold any lessons for the United States. With its 251 inmates, Halden is one of Norway's largest prisons, in a country with only 3,800 prisoners (according to the International Center for Prison Studies); by contrast, in the United States, the average number is around 1,300 at maximum-security prisons, with a total of 2.2 million incarcerated (according to the federal Bureau of Justice Statistics). Halden's rehabilitation programs seem logistically and financially out of reach for such a system to even contemplate.

And yet there was a brief historical moment in which the United States pondered a similar approach to criminal justice. As part of his "war on crime," Lyndon B. Johnson established the President's Commission on Law Enforcement and Administration of Justice, a body of 19 advisers appointed to study, among other things, the conditions and practices of catastrophically overstretched prisons. The resulting 1967 report, "The Challenge of Crime in a Free Society," expressed concern that many correctional institutions were detrimental to rehabilitation: "Life in many institutions is at best barren and futile, at worst unspeakably brutal and degrading. ... The conditions in which they live are the poorest possible preparation for their successful re-entry into society, and often merely reinforce in them a pattern of manipulation and destructiveness." And in its recommendations, the commission put forward a vision for prisons that would be surprisingly like Halden. "Architecturally, the model institution would resemble as much as possible a normal residential setting. Rooms, for example, would have doors rather than bars. Inmates would eat at small tables in an informal atmosphere. There would be classrooms, recreation facilities, day rooms, and perhaps a shop and library."

In the mid-1970s, the federal Bureau of Prisons completed three pretrial detention facilities that were designed to reflect those best practices. The three Metropolitan Correctional Centers, or M.C.C.s, were the first of what would come to be known as "new generation" institutions. The results, in both architecture and operation, were a radical departure from previous models. Groups of 44 prisoners populated self-contained units in which all of the single-inmate cells (with wooden doors meant to reduce both noise and cost) opened onto a day room, where they ate, socialized and met with visitors or counselors, minimizing the need for moving inmates outside the unit. All the prisoners spent the entire day outside their cells with a single unarmed correctional officer in an environment meant to diminish the sense of institutionalization and its attendant psychological stresses, with wooden and upholstered furniture, desks in the cells, porcelain toilets, exposed light fixtures, brightly colored walls, skylights and carpeted floors.

But by the time the centers opened, public and political commitment to rehabilitation programs in American prisons had shifted. Much of the backlash within penological circles can be traced to Robert Martinson, a sociology researcher at the City University of New York. In a 1974 article for the journal Public Interest, he summarized an analysis of data from 1945 to 1967 about the impact of rehabilitation programs on recidivism. Despite the fact that around half the individual programs did show evidence of effectiveness in reducing recidivism, Martinson's article concluded that no category of rehabilitation program (education or psychotherapy, for example) showed consistent results across prison systems. "With few and isolated exceptions," he wrote, "the rehabilitative efforts that have been reported so far have had no appreciable effect on recidivism." Martinson's paper was immediately seized upon by the news media and politicians, who latched on to the idea that "nothing works" in regard to prisoner rehabilitation. "It Doesn't Work" was the title of a "60 Minutes" segment on rehabilitation. "They don't rehabilitate, they don't deter, they don't punish and they don't protect," Jerry Brown, the governor of California, said in a 1975 speech. A top psychiatrist for the Bureau of Prisons resigned in disgust at what he perceived to be an abandonment of commitment to rehabilitation. At the dedication ceremony for the San Diego M.C.C. in 1974, one of the very structures designed with rehabilitation in mind, William Saxbe, the attorney general of the United States, declared that the ability of a correctional program to produce rehabilitation was a "myth" for all but the youngest offenders.

Martinson's paper was quickly challenged; a 1975 analysis of much of the same data by another sociologist criticized Martinson's choice to overlook the successful programs and their characteristics in favor of a broad conclusion devoid of context. By 1979, in light of new analyses, Martinson published another paper that unequivocally withdrew his previous conclusion, declaring that "contrary to my previous position, some treatment programs do have an appreciable effect on recidivism." But by then, the "nothing works" narrative was firmly entrenched. In

1984, a Senate report calling for more stringent sentencing guidelines cited Martinson's 1974 paper, without acknowledging his later reversal. The tough-on-crime policies that sprouted in Congress and state legislatures soon after included mandatory minimums, longer sentences, three-strikes laws, legislation allowing juveniles to be prosecuted as adults and an increase in prisoners' "maxing out," or being released without passing through reintegration programs or the parole system. Between 1975 and 2005, the rate of incarceration in the United States skyrocketed, from roughly 100 inmates per 100,000 citizens to more than 700 — consistently one of the highest rates in the world. Though Americans make up about only 4.6 percent of the world's population, American prisons hold 22 percent of all incarcerated people.

Today, the M.C.C. model of incarceration, which is now known as "direct supervision," is not entirely dead. Around 350 facilities — making up less than 7 percent of the incarceration sites in the United States, mostly county-level jails, which are pretrial and short-stay institutions — have been built on the direct-supervision model and are, with greater and lesser fidelity to the ideal, run by the same principles of inmate management developed for the new-generation prisons of the 1970s. The body of data from those jails over the last 40 years has shown that they have lower levels of violence among inmates and against guards and reduced recidivism; some of these institutions, when directly compared with the older facilities they replaced, saw drops of 90 percent in violent incidents. But extrapolating from this tiny group of facilities to the entire nation, and in particular to its maximum-security prisons, is an impossible thought experiment. Much about the American culture of imprisonment today — the training of guards, the acculturation of prisoners, the incentives of politicians, the inattention of citizens — would have to change for the Norwegian approach to gain anything more than a minor foothold in the correctional system. The country has gone down a different road during the past half century, and that road does not lead to Halden Fengsel.

EVEN UNDERSTANDING HOW well the Norwegian approach works in Norway is a difficult business. On a Saturday afternoon in Oslo, I met Ragnar Kristoffersen, an anthropologist who teaches at the Correctional Service of Norway Staff Academy, which trains correction officers. Kristoffersen published a research paper comparing recidivism rates in the Scandinavian countries. A survey of inmates who were released in 2005 put Norway's two-year recidivism rate at 20 percent, the lowest in Scandinavia, which was widely praised in the Norwegian and international press. For comparison, a 2014 recidivism report from the United States Bureau of Justice Statistics announced that an estimated 68 percent of prisoners released in 30 states in 2005 were arrested for a new crime within three years.

I asked Kristoffersen if he had spent time at Halden. He reached into his briefcase and pulled out a handful of printed sheets. "Have you seen this?" he asked while waving them at me. "It's preposterous!" They were printouts of English-language articles about the prison, the most offensive and misleading lines highlighted. He read a few quotes about the prison's architecture and furnishings to me with disgust. I acknowledged that the hyperbolic descriptions would catch the attention of American and British readers, for whom the cost of a prison like Halden would probably need to be justified by strong evidence of a significant reduction in recidivism.

Somewhat to my surprise, Kristoffersen went into a rant about the unreliability of recidivism statistics for evaluating corrections practices. From one local, state or national justice system to another, diverse and ever-changing policies and practices in sentencing — what kinds and lengths of sentences judges impose for what types of crimes, how likely they are to reincarcerate an offender for a technical violation of parole, how much emphasis they put on community sentences over prison terms and many other factors — make it nearly impossible to know if you're comparing apples to apples. Kristoffersen pointed out that in 2005, Norway was putting people in prison for traffic offenses like speeding, something that few other countries do. Speeders are at low risk for reoffending and receiving another prison sentence for that crime or any other. Excluding traffic offenders, Norway's recidivism rate would, per that survey, be around 25 percent after two years.

Then there was the question of what qualifies as "recidivism." Some countries and states count any new arrest as recidivism, while others count only new convictions or new prison sentences; still others include parole violations. The numbers most commonly cited in news reports about recidivism, like the 20 percent celebrated by Norway or the 68 percent lamented by the United States, begin to fall apart on closer inspection. That 68 percent, for example, is a three-year number, but digging into the report shows the more comparable two-year rate to be 60 percent. And that number reflects not reincarceration (the basis for the Norwegian statistic) but rearrest, a much wider net. Fifteen pages into the Bureau of Justice Statistics report, I found a two-year reincarceration rate, probably the best available comparison to Norway's measures. Kristoffersen's caveat in mind, that translated to a much less drastic contrast: Norway, 25 percent; the United States, 28.8 percent.

What does that mean? Is the American prison system doing a better job than conventional wisdom would suggest? It is frustratingly hard to tell. I asked Kristoffersen if that low reincarceration rate might reflect the fact that long prison sentences mean that many prisoners become naturally less likely to reoffend because of advanced age. He agreed that was possible, along with many other more and less obvious variables. It turned out that measuring the effectiveness of Halden in particular was nearly impossible; Norway's recidivism statistics are broken down by prison of release, and almost no prisoners are released directly from maximum-security prisons, so Halden doesn't have a recidivism number.

After nearly an hour of talking about the finer points of statistics, though, Kristoffersen stopped and made a point that wasn't about statistics at all.

"You have to be aware — there's a logical type of error which is common in debating these things," he said. "That is, you shouldn't mix two kinds of principles. The one is about: How do you fight crimes? How do you reduce recidivism? And the other is: What are the principles of humanity that you want to build your system on? They are two different questions."

He leaned back in his chair and went on. "We like to think that treating inmates nicely, humanely, is good for the rehabilitation. And I'm not arguing against it. I'm saying two things. There are poor evidence saying that treating people nicely will keep them from committing new crimes. Very poor evidence."

He paused. "But then again, my second point would be," he said, "if you treat people badly, it's a reflection on yourself." In officer-training school, he explained, guards are taught that treating inmates humanely is something they should do not for the inmates but for themselves. The theory is that if officers are taught to be harsh, domineering and suspicious, it will ripple outward in their lives, affecting their self-image, their families, even Norway as a whole. Kristoffersen cited a line that is usually attributed to Dostoyevsky: "The degree of civilization in a society can be judged by entering its prisons."

I heard the same quotation from Are Hoidal, Halden's warden, not long before I left Halden. He told me proudly that people wanted to work at the prison, and officers and teachers told me that they hoped to spend their whole careers at Halden, that they were proud of making a difference.

"They make big changes in here," Hoidal said as we made our way through the succession of doors that would return us to the world outside. There was, improbably, an actual rainbow stretching from the clouds above, landing somewhere outside the wall. Hoidal was quiet for a moment, then laughed. "I have the best job in the world!" He chuckled and shook his head. He sounded surprised.

JESSICA BENKO is a print and radio journalist whose work has appeared in National Geographic and Wired and on "This American Life."

Could Restorative Justice Fix the Internet?

OPINION | BY CHARLIE WARZEL | AUG. 20, 2019

Perhaps. But it relies on people being capable of shame, so . . .

AS WE ALL SPEND our days yelling at one another online, it's easy to despair and wonder: Is there any way to fix our toxic internet?

Micah Loewinger, a producer for WNYC's "On the Media," was pondering this question when he met Lindsay Blackwell, a Ph.D. student at the University of Michigan who studies online harassment. Ms. Blackwell, also a researcher at Facebook, had been toying with the idea of applying the principles of the restorative justice movement to online content moderation.

Restorative justice is an alternative form of criminal justice that focuses on mediation. Often, an offender will meet with the victim and the broader community with a chance to make amends. The confrontation, advocates of the technique argue, helps the offender come to terms with the crime while giving the victim a chance to be heard. If the relationship is repaired and the harm to the victim reduced, the offender is allowed to re-enter the community. Studies, including one by the Department of Justice, suggest the approach can be an effective way to decrease repeat offenses and works for perpetrators and victims.

For Ms. Blackwell, applying a similar tactic to tech platforms made sense. Current tech company enforcements, if enacted, tend to be harsh and geared toward deterrence, not treating the underlying causes of rule-breaking behavior.

Ms. Blackwell and Mr. Loewinger decided to run what they called "a highly unscientific" experiment on Reddit, a social network with tens of thousands of forum communities. Each community is policed by volunteer moderators who take down offensive posts and enforce that community's set of rules. Ms. Blackwell and Mr. Loewinger teamed up with the moderators of Reddit's r/Christianity community, which has roughly 200,000 members. It is diverse, comprising L.G.B.T.Q. Christians, fundamentalists, atheists and others with an interest in posting about the faith. Discussions get intense.

The pair selected three users who were barred for repeatedly violating rules. They created a chat room where the offender and community moderator would meet with Mr. Loewinger and Ms. Blackwell, who acted as mediators. The offenders would be confronted with past bad behavior and given the opportunity to better understand why they were barred. Upon successful completion, they'd be readmitted to the group.

The results were mixed. In one case, mediation broke down, in part because of Ms. Blackwell and Mr. Loewinger's inexperience mediating and tensions between a user and a moderator that boiled over. The second case, which involved an anti-gay user who was accused of bullying an L.G.B.T.Q. user into committing suicide years ago, proved simply too toxic to continue. The third case, involving "James," an atheist and biblical historian who was barred for repeatedly violating r/Christianity's rules for civil discussion, was a success.

At various points throughout the chat log of the mediation, James expressed genuine shock. "Dang this wasn't the context that I remembered," he types at one point, after looking at past bullying posts. "I thought someone else was the instigator and I felt ganged-up on or something. But ... looks like I was the instigator." He apologized for lashing out, at one point suggesting "the problem is more obviously about (mis)communication and hostility that comes up in the course of these conversations." Eventually, the moderators lifted their ban.

When I spoke to James over the phone about the process, he described his aggressive behavior as a kind of dissociation — a moment of weakness where he stopped seeing those on the other end of the thread as real people. "My frustration expressed itself as insult diarrhea with no regard to whether I was being reasonable," he said. He noted that he'd been back in the community for two months, is more conscious of his interactions and has yet to break the rules.

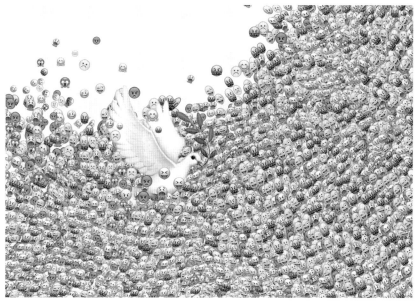

James isn't convinced the process could work for everyone. He argued that mediation was effective for his specific personality type. "It's the element of shame," he said. "I'm somebody who feels guilt being confronted and it allowed me to see I was the one at fault." Ms. Blackwell and Mr. Loewinger's mixed results suggest success is far from guaranteed. Online, mediators have to deal with pseudonymous individuals, trolls and pranksters with no desire to reform. Even those dealing in good faith might bristle at having to apologize or confront their victims. Given the nature of online harassment and bullying, the restorative justice approach is full of pitfalls. Forcing targeted minorities or vulnerable users to confront abusers, for one, could increase trauma or put undue burden on victims.

Most daunting is the issue of scale. There's simply no way to replicate the amount of time and effort involved with Ms. Blackwell and Mr. Loewinger's experiment across the web. "It's like trying to moderate a wild river," an r/Christianity moderator said in the chat logs. "It's only getting worse, too. I can't even begin to evaluate all of this stuff." The ceaseless torrent of posts and comments is why tech platforms are increasingly turning to algorithms and artificial intelligence to solve the problem.

But successful moderation — the kind that not only keeps a community from collapsing under the weight of its own toxicity but also creates a healthy forum — requires a human touch. Even skilled moderators assume a huge psychological burden; many working for Facebook and YouTube are outside contractors, subjected daily to torrents of psychologically traumatizing content and almost always without proper resources. Even in small communities, keeping the peace requires a herculean effort. A recent New Yorker article described the job of two human moderators of a midsize tech-news message board as an act of "relentless patience and good faith."

This reality makes Ms. Blackwell and Mr. Loewinger's experiment equal parts compelling and dispiriting. Mr. Loewinger remains optimistic. "It's easy to write off all people who exhibit jerk-ish behavior online as pathological trolls," he told me. "Dislodging that assumption might hold the key to a less toxic web. The James case demonstrated to me that people are open to reflecting on what they've done, especially when treated with dignity." Ms. Blackwell argued that having reformed users back in the community actually makes the forums healthier. "We will never effectively reduce online harassment unless we address the underlying motivations for participating in abusive behavior, and having reformed violators go on to model prosocial norms is an incredible bonus," she said.

But if reform means an abundance of shame and dignity on the internet, it's hard not to feel that all is already lost. Still, the pair's earnestness is refreshing. And at its core there's a lesson: If fast, scalable algorithmic solutions gave us the broken system we've got, it's stripped-down patience and humanity that have the best chance of pulling us out.

CHARLIE WARZEL, a New York Times Opinion writer at large, covers technology, media, politics and online extremism.

CHAPTER 5

Abolition: A Vision of Nonviolent Justice

In criminal justice reform conversations, one of the hardest questions is what the purpose of prisons should be. One argument is for prison abolition. That position believes prisons cause more harm than they prevent, have an underlying racist intent and should be replaced with resources devoted to community well-being. While obviously not a consensus view, prison abolition puts restorative justice in a historical and political context, where we take seriously the harms that prisons have caused.

Why Are American Prisons So Afraid of This Book?

BY JONAH ENGEL BROMWICH | JAN. 18, 2018

IN THE EIGHT YEARS since its publication, "The New Jim Crow," a book by Michelle Alexander that explores the phenomenon of mass incarceration, has sold well over a million copies, been compared to the work of W.E.B. Du Bois, been cited in the legal decisions to end stop-and-frisk and sentencing laws, and been quoted passionately on stage at the Academy Awards.

But for the more than 130,000 adults in prison in North Carolina and Florida, the book is strictly off-limits.

And prisoners around the country often have trouble obtaining copies of the book, which points to the vast racial disparities in sentencing policy, and the way that mass incarceration has ravaged the African-American population.

This month, after protests, New Jersey revoked a ban some of its prisons had placed on the book, while New York quickly scrapped a program that would have limited its inmates' ability to receive books at all.

Ms. Alexander, a civil rights lawyer and former clerk on the Supreme Court, said the barriers to reading the book are no accident.

"Some prison officials are determined to keep the people they lock in cages as ignorant as possible about the racial, social and political forces that have made the United States the most punitive nation on earth," she said. "Perhaps they worry the truth might actually set the captives free."

A spokeswoman for the Florida Department of Corrections confirmed that the book had been banned but would not elaborate. A form from the prison system's literature review committee obtained by The New York Times indicates that the book was rejected because it presented a security threat and was filled with what the document called "racial overtures."

In North Carolina prisons, "The New Jim Crow" has been banned multiple times, most recently on Feb. 24, 2017, when it was deemed "likely to provoke confrontation between racial groups." State policy dictates that such bans can last for only a year, so the book will be permitted in the state's prisons late next month — unless it is banned again.

"All you need is one prison to challenge it, and then the book goes back on the list," said Katya Roytburd, a volunteer with Prison Books Collective, a nonprofit that sends free books to prisoners in North Carolina and Alabama.

The central thesis of "The New Jim Crow" is that the mass incarceration of black people is an extension of the American tradition of racial discrimination.

It zeroes in on how the "law and order" rhetoric of the 1950s and 1960s led to the war on drugs and harsh law enforcement and sentencing policies, which disproportionately affect black people.

Michelle Alexander in 2012. Her book on mass incarceration, "The New Jim Crow," has been banned by prisons in North Carolina and Florida.

"It is no longer socially permissible to use race, explicitly, as a justification for discrimination, exclusion, and social contempt," she writes in the introduction. "So we don't. Rather than rely on race we use our criminal justice system to label people of color 'criminals' and then engage in all the practices we supposedly left behind."

Black people are still imprisoned at over five times the rate of white people, according to a 2016 report by The Sentencing Project, a prison reform advocacy group. And while a bipartisan push for sentencing reform took place during President Barack Obama's second term, those efforts have stalled under Attorney General Jeff Sessions and President Trump.

The choices prisons make when banning books can seem arbitrary, even capricious. In Texas, 10,000 titles are banned, including such head-scratchers as "The Color Purple" and a compilation by the humor writer Dave Barry.

"Mein Kampf," on the other hand, is permitted, along with several books by white nationalists, despite the existence of prison gangs like the murderous Aryan Brotherhood of Texas.

"When you look at the banned book lists and specifically the stuff that's being allowed, there's a definite bias toward violent armed white supremacy and the censorship of anything that questions the existing religious or political status quo," said Paul Wright, the executive director of the Human Rights Defense Center.

Activists see bans as an indictment of how prisoners are limited more broadly. Amy Peterson, a member of NYC Books Through Bars, which sends books to inmates in 40 states, said books were often sent back with little explanation.

"It does seem very much up to the person in the shipping room who's making these arbitrary decisions," she said. "I see it as one of the many ways that people are deprived of basic rights in prison."

But for many incarcerated people, the ban on "The New Jim Crow" does not seem arbitrary. In 2014, Dominic Passmore, a prisoner in Michigan, ordered the book after checking to make sure that it had not been banned in the state. When it arrived, according to state documents, the prison's mailroom staff refused to give it to him, citing its racial content.

Months later, after a series of appeals, the state decided that Mr. Passmore could read the book but informed him that he would have to buy a new copy, as it had misplaced his.

Mr. Passmore, who spent nine years behind bars after pleading no contest to armed robbery charges when he was 14, eventually read the book. He said that it opened his eyes to the wrongs done to black people.

"I feel like the reason why they tried to reject it is because they didn't want me to have that kind of knowledge," said Mr. Passmore, who was recently released.

Prison officials almost universally agree that certain books should be prohibited. Roger Werholtz, who served as secretary of corrections in Kansas and as interim executive director of corrections in Colorado, said that books that could interfere with safety, like instructions on how to pick locks or make weapons, or those that could incite disturbances, such as racist or white supremacist literature, were banned under his watch.

He said that he did not think banning Ms. Alexander's book for its arguments about race made sense.

"I would be pretty skeptical of that," he said. "That's not anything that you don't see in the newspaper. Frankly, most prison officials talk very openly about the overrepresentation of minorities."

Jason Hernandez, 40, was a 21-year-old first-time, nonviolent drug offender when he was convicted of conspiracy to distribute crack cocaine. He was sentenced to life imprisonment without parole.

Mr. Hernandez studied law in prison and filed his own appeals, only to see them denied. In 2010, he borrowed "The New Jim Crow" from the prison's library lending program.

It inspired him to start a grass-roots organization to help himself and other nonviolent drug offenders with life sentences. In September 2011, he appealed directly to Mr. Obama for clemency. His request was granted and he was released in 2015.

"They prevent books from going in there that could maybe help people escape," he said. "This is what this book did for me, and what it's done for hundreds of others."

Reckoning With Violence

OPINION | BY MICHELLE ALEXANDER | MARCH 3, 2019

We must face violent crime honestly and courageously if we are ever to end mass incarceration and provide survivors what they truly want and need to heal.

WHEN CHICAGO'S POLICE CHIEF, Eddie Johnson, looked out at the sea of journalists to share the breaking news that Jussie Smollett, a well-known and beloved actor, had allegedly staged a violent racist and homophobic attack against himself, he said with great emotion: "Guys, I look out into the crowd, I just wish that the families of gun violence in this city got this much attention."

Chicago is besieged by horrific levels of violence, including thousands of shootings and hundreds of homicides each year. More than 500 people were killed in 2018, down from 664 in 2017. This ongoing tragedy cannot be blamed on any lack of aggressiveness on the part of law enforcement. Indeed, if wars on crime and drugs, militarized policing, "get tough" sentencing policies, torture of suspects, and perpetual monitoring and surveillance of the poorest, most crime-ridden communities actually worked to keep people safe, Chicago would be one of the safest cities in the world.

Despite the abysmal failure of "get tough" strategies to break cycles of violence in cities like Chicago, reformers of our criminal justice system in recent years have largely avoided the subject of violence, instead focusing their energy and resources on overhauling our nation's drug laws and reducing penalties for nonviolent offenses.

It's not difficult to understand why. After all, violent crime was used by politicians for decades to rationalize "get tough" rhetoric, declarations of war, harsh mandatory minimum sentencing, and a prison-building boom unlike anything the world has ever seen. The tide has turned somewhat, but reformers are proceeding cautiously, reaching first for the low-hanging fruit.

Drug law reform has never been an easier sell — especially now that opioid addiction is perceived as ravaging primarily white communities, generating far more compassion than black communities ever experienced during the crack epidemic in the late 1980s. The opportunity to curb the drug war is critically important for many communities of color, especially in places like Chicago where it has caused catastrophic harm. Nationally, the drug war helped to birth our system of mass incarceration, which now governs not only the 2.2 million people who are locked in prisons and jails in this country, but also the 4.5 million people that are under correctional control outside prison walls — on probation or parole. More than 70 million people now have criminal records that authorize legal discrimination against them, relegating them to a permanent second-class status. The overwhelming majority ensnared by this system have been convicted of nonviolent crimes and drug offenses.

And yet, as Danielle Sered points out in her profoundly necessary book, "Until We Reckon," if we fail to face violence in our communities honestly, courageously and with profound compassion for the survivors — many of whom are also perpetrators of harm — our nation will never break its addiction to caging human beings.

Fifty-four percent of the people currently held in state prisons have been convicted of a crime classified as violent. We will never slash our prison population by 50 percent — the goal of a number of current campaigns — much less get back to levels of incarceration that we had before the race to incarcerate began in the early 1980s, without addressing the one issue most reformers avoid: violence.

Reckoning with violence in a meaningful way does not mean "getting tough" in the way that phrase has been used for decades; nor does it mean being "smart on crime" to the extent that phrase has become shorthand for being "tough" on violent crime but "soft" on nonviolent crime — a formulation that continues to be embraced by some so-called "progressive prosecutors" today.

As Ms. Sered explains in her book, drawing on her experience working with hundreds of survivors and perpetrators of violence in Brooklyn and the Bronx, imprisonment isn't just an inadequate tool; it's often enormously counterproductive — leaving survivors and their communities worse off.

Survivors themselves know this. That's why fully 90 percent of survivors in New York City, when given the chance to choose whether they want the person who harmed them incarcerated or in a restorative justice process — one that offers support to survivors while empowering them to help decide how perpetrators of violence can repair the damage they've done — choose the latter and opt to use the services of Ms. Sered's nonprofit organization, Common Justice.

Ms. Sered launched Common Justice in an effort to give survivors of violence — like herself — a meaningful pathway to accountability without perpetuating the harms endemic to mass incarceration. As a restorative justice program, it offers a survivor-centered accountability process that "gives those directly impacted by acts of violence the opportunity to shape what repair will look like, and, in the case of the responsible party, to carry out that repair instead of going to prison." The people who choose to participate are victims of serious violent felonies — people who have been shot, stabbed or robbed — and who decide that they would prefer to get answers from the person who harmed them, be heard in a restorative justice circle, help to devise an accountability plan, and receive comprehensive victim services, rather than send the person who harmed them to prison.

Ninety percent is a stunning figure considering everything we've been led to believe that survivors actually want. For years, we've been told that victims of violence want nothing more than for the people who hurt them to be locked up and treated harshly. It is true that some survivors do want revenge or retribution, especially in the immediate aftermath of the crime. Ms. Sered is emphatic that rage is not pathological and a desire for revenge is not blameworthy; both are normal and can be important to the healing process, much as denial and anger are normal stages of grief.

But she also stresses that the number of people who are interested only in revenge or punishment is greatly exaggerated. After all, survivors are almost never offered real choices. Usually when we ask victims "Do you want incarceration?" what we're really asking is "Do you want something or nothing?" And when any of us are hurt, and when our families and communities are hurting, we want *something* rather than nothing. In many oppressed communities, drug treatment, good schools, economic investment, job training, trauma and grief support are not available options. Restorative justice is not an option. The only thing on offer is prisons, prosecutors and police.

But what happens, Ms. Sered wondered, if instead of asking, "Do you want something or nothing?" we started asking "Do you want this intervention or that prison?" It turns out, when given a real choice, very few survivors choose prison as their preferred response.

This is not because survivors, as a group, are especially merciful. To the contrary, they're pragmatic. They know the criminal justice system will almost certainly fail to deliver what they want and need most to overcome their pain and trauma. More than 95 percent of cases end in plea bargains negotiated by lawyers behind the scenes. Given the system's design, survivors know the system cannot be trusted to validate their suffering, give them answers or even a meaningful opportunity to be heard. Nor can it be trusted to keep them or others safe.

In fact, many victims find that incarceration actually makes them feel less safe. They worry that others will be angry with them for reporting the crime and retaliate, or fear what will happen when the person eventually returns home. Many believe, for good reason, that incarceration will likely make the person worse, not better — a frightening prospect when they're likely to encounter the person again when they're back in the neighborhood.

As one woman whose 14-year-old son had been badly beaten and robbed explained to Ms. Sered, "When I first found out about this, I wanted the young man to drown to death. And then I wanted him to burn to death. And then I realized as a mother that I don't want either of those things. I want him to drown in a river of fire." But when she reflected on the fact that the young man who harmed her son would eventually return home from prison and cross paths with her children again, she said, "I have to ask myself: When that day comes, do I want that young man to have been upstate or do I want him to have been with y'all?"

The restorative circle, a meeting during which responsible parties sit with those they have harmed (or surrogates who take their place), a trained facilitator, and people who support both parties, is central to the process. It offers those affected by a crime with the power and opportunity to ask questions, as well as describe their needs and the ways they've been harmed. Ultimately, the parties strive to reach agreement about what the responsible party can do to make things as right as possible. The circle can be transformative for both survivors and those who've caused harm. In Ms. Sered's experience, survivors not only want answers to factual questions, they want acknowledgment of their suffering and the moral wrongs. They want to be able to say: "How dare you? My brother was killed the year before you stabbed me. Can you imagine how it felt to my mother to get the call from the hospital that I was unconscious in the E.R. and had been stabbed?" Sered explains.

Witnessing the pain and anguish of survivors, and taking full responsibility for what they've done by committing to specific actions to repair themselves and others, has a far greater impact on those who've committed harm than we might imagine. One young man, who had been a gang member since he was 8 years old, could not leave the building after participating in a restorative circle with Common Justice because he was shaking so badly after admitting the harm he had done. He asked staff members, "Can I stay in your office for a few minutes before I leave?" When asked to explain, he said, "You know, for all I've done and all that's been done to me, I don't know if I've ever heard a real apology before. Do you think I did all right? Pardon my language, that is the scariest shit I ever did."

A growing body of research strongly supports the anecdotal evidence that restorative justice programs increase the odds of safety, reduce recidivism and alleviate trauma. "Until We Reckon" cites studies showing that survivors report 80 to 90 percent rates of satisfaction with restorative processes, as compared to 30 percent for traditional court systems.

Common Justice's success rate is high: Only 7 percent of responsible parties have been terminated from the program for a new crime. And it's not alone in successfully applying restorative justice principles. Numerous organizations — such as Community Justice for Youth Institute and Project NIA in Chicago; the Insight Prison Project in San Quentin; the Community Conferencing Center in Baltimore; and Restorative Justice for Oakland Youth — are doing so in communities, schools, and criminal justice settings from coast-to-coast.

In 2016, the Alliance for Safety and Justice conducted the first national poll of crime survivors and the results are consistent with the emerging trend toward restorative justice. The majority said they "believe that time in prison makes people more likely to commit another crime rather than less likely." Sixty-nine percent preferred holding people accountable through options beyond prison, such as mental health treatment, substance abuse treatment, rehabilitation, community supervision and public service. Survivors' support for alternatives to incarceration was even higher than among the general public.

Survivors are right to question incarceration as a strategy for violence reduction. Violence is driven by shame, exposure to violence, isolation and an inability to meet one's economic needs — all of which are core features of imprisonment. Perhaps most importantly, according to Ms. Sered, "Nearly everyone who has committed violence first survived it," and studies indicate that experiencing violence is the greater predictor of committing it. Caging and isolating a person who's already been damaged by violence is hardly a recipe for positive transformation.

That said, Ms. Sered makes clear that she doesn't believe that having been a victim of crime excuses acts of violence in any way: "When we hurt someone, we incur an obligation. Period." In fact, it seems her greatest complaint about our system of mass incarceration is that it fails to take accountability seriously. Our criminal injustice system lets people off the hook, as they aren't obligated to answer the victims' questions, listen to them, honor their pain, express genuine remorse, or do what they can to repair the harm they've done. They're not required to take steps to heal themselves or address their own trauma, so they're less likely to harm others in the future. The only thing prison requires is that people stay in their cages and somehow endure the isolation and violence of captivity. Prison deprives everyone concerned — victims and those who have caused harm, as well as impacted families and communities — the opportunity to heal, honor their own humanity, and to break cycles of violence that have destroyed far too many lives.

Ms. Sered acknowledges that we, as a society, are not yet prepared to apply restorative and transformative justice principles to all crimes of violence. Some people do need to be separated in order to keep others safe. But if we invest our resources in the healing, restoration and rebuilding of relationships and communities — and stop pretending that caging people on a massive scale makes our communities safer — we just might discover that we are capable of reckoning with one another.

MICHELLE ALEXANDER became a New York Times columnist in 2018. She is a civil rights lawyer and advocate, legal scholar and author of "The New Jim Crow: Mass Incarceration in the Age of Colorblindness."

Is Prison Necessary? Ruth Wilson Gilmore Might Change Your Mind

BY RACHEL KUSHNER | APRIL 17, 2019

In three decades of advocating for prison abolition, the activist and scholar has helped transform how people think about criminal justice.

THERE'S AN ANECDOTE that Ruth Wilson Gilmore likes to share about being at an environmental-justice conference in Fresno in 2003. People from all over California's Central Valley had gathered to talk about the serious environmental hazards their communities faced, mostly as a result of decades of industrial farming, conditions that still have not changed. (The air quality in the Central Valley is the worst in the nation, and one million of its residents drink tap water more poisoned than the water in Flint, Mich.) There was a "youth track" at the conference, in which children were meant to talk about their worries and then decide as a group what was most important to be done in the name of environmental justice. Gilmore, a renowned geography professor (then at University of California, Berkeley, now at the CUNY Graduate Center in Manhattan) and an influential figure in the prison-abolition movement, was a keynote speaker.

She was preparing her talk when someone told her that the kids wanted to speak with her. She went into the room where they were gathered. The children were primarily Latino, many of them the sons and daughters of farmworkers or other people in the agriculture industry. They ranged in age, but most were middle schoolers: old enough to have strong opinions and to distrust adults. They were frowning at her with their shoulders up and their arms crossed. She didn't know these kids, but she understood that they were against her.

"What's going on?" she asked.

"We hear you're a prison abolitionist," one said. "You want to close prisons?"

Gilmore said that was right; she did want to close prisons.

But why, they asked. And before she could answer, one said, "But what about the people who do something seriously wrong?" Others chimed in. "What about people who hurt other people?" "What about if someone kills someone?"

Whether from tiny farm towns or from public housing around Fresno and Bakersfield, these children, it was obvious to Gilmore, understood innately the harshness of the world and were not going to be easily persuaded.

"I get where you're coming from," she said. "But how about this: Instead of asking whether anyone should be locked up or go free, why don't we think about why we solve problems by repeating the kind of behavior that brought us the problem in the first place?" She was asking them to consider why, as a society, we would choose to model cruelty and vengeance.

As she spoke, she felt the kids icing her out, as if she were a new teacher who had come to proffer some bogus argument and tell them it was for their own good. But Gilmore pressed on, determined. She told them that in Spain, where it's really quite rare for one person to kill another, the average time you might serve for murdering someone is seven years.

"What? Seven years!" The kids were in such disbelief about a seven-year sentence for murder that they relaxed a little bit. They could be outraged about that, instead of about Gilmore's ideas.

Gilmore told them that in the unusual event that someone in Spain thinks he is going to solve a problem by killing another person, the response is that the person loses seven years of his life to think about what he has done, and to figure out how to live when released. "What this policy tells me," she said, "is that where life is precious, life *is* precious." Which is to say, she went on, in Spain people have decided that life has enough value that they are not going to behave in a punitive and violent and life-annihilating way toward people who hurt people. "And what this demonstrates is that for people trying to solve their everyday problems, behaving in a violent and life-annihilating way is not a solution."

The children showed Gilmore no emotion except guarded doubt, expressed in side eye. She kept talking. She believed her own arguments and had given them many years of thought as an activist and a scholar, but the kids were a tough sell. They told Gilmore that they would think about what she said and dismissed her. As she left the room, she felt totally defeated.

At the end of the day, the kids made a presentation to the broader conference, announcing, to Gilmore's surprise, that in their workshop they had come to the conclusion that there were three environmental hazards that affected their lives most pressingly as children growing up in the Central Valley. Those hazards were pesticides, the police and prisons.

"Sitting there listening to the kids stopped my heart," Gilmore told me. "Why? Abolition is deliberately everything-ist; it's about the entirety of human-environmental relations. So, when I gave the kids an example from a different place, I worried they might conclude that some people elsewhere were just better or kinder than people in the South San Joaquin Valley — in other words, they'd decide what happened elsewhere was irrelevant to their lives. But judging from their presentation, the kids lifted up the larger point of what I'd tried to share: Where life is precious, life is precious. They asked themselves, 'Why do we feel every day that life here is *not* precious?' In trying to answer, they identified what makes them vulnerable."

PRISON ABOLITION, as a movement, sounds provocative and absolute, but what it is as a practice requires subtler understanding. For Gilmore, who has been active in the movement for more than 30 years, it's both a long-term goal and a practical policy program, calling for government investment in jobs, education, housing, health care — all the elements that are required for a productive and violence-free life. Abolition means not just the closing of prisons but the presence, instead, of vital systems of support that many communities lack. Instead of asking how, in a future without prisons, we will deal with so-called violent people, abolitionists ask how we resolve inequalities and get people the resources they need long before the hypothetical moment when, as Gilmore puts it, they "mess up."

"Every age has had its hopes," William Morris wrote in 1885, "hopes that look to something beyond the life of the age itself, hopes that try to pierce into the future." Morris was a proto-abolitionist: In his utopian novel "News From Nowhere," there are no prisons, and this is treated as an obvious, necessary condition for a happy society.

In Morris's era, the prison was relatively new as the most common form of punishment. In England, historically, people were incarcerated for only a short time, before being dragged out and whipped in the street. As Angela Davis narrates in her 2003 book, "Are Prisons Obsolete?" while early English common law deemed the crime of petty treason punishable by being burned alive, by 1790 this punishment was reformed to death by hanging. In the wake of the Enlightenment, European reformers gradually moved away from corporal punishment *tout court*; people would go to prison for a set period of time, rather than to wait for the punishment to come. The penitentiary movement in both England and the United States in the early 19th century was motivated in part by the demand for more humanitarian punishment. Prison was the reform.

If prison, in its philosophical origin, was meant as a humane alternative to beatings or torture or death, it has transformed into a fixed feature of modern life, one that is not known, even by its supporters and administrators, for its humanity. In the United States, we now have more than two million incarcerated people, a majority of them black or brown, virtually all of them from poor communities. Prisons not only have violated human rights and failed at rehabilitation; it's not even clear that prisons deter crime or increase public safety.

Following an incarceration boom that began all over the United States around 1980 and only recently started to level off, reform has become politically popular. But abolitionists argue that many reforms have done little more than reinforce the system. In every state where the death penalty has been abolished, for example, it has been replaced by the sentence of life without parole — to many people a death sentence by other, more protracted means. Another product of good intentions: campaigns to reform indeterminate sentencing, resulting in three-strike programs and mandatory-minimum sentencing, which traded one cruelty for another. Over all, reforms have not significantly reduced incarceration numbers, and no recent reform legislation has even aspired to do so.

For instance, the first federal prison reform in almost 10 years, the bipartisan First Step Act, which President Trump signed into law late last year, will result in the release of only some 7,000 of the 2.3 million people currently locked up when it goes into effect. Federal legislation pertains only to federal prisons, which hold less than 10 percent of the nation's prison population, and of those, First Step applies to only a slim subset. As Gilmore said to me, noting an outsize public enthusiasm after the act passed the Senate, "There are people who behave as though the origin and cure are federal. So many are unaware of how the country is juridically organized, and that there are at least 52 criminal-legal jurisdictions in the U.S."

Which isn't to say that Gilmore and other abolitionists are opposed to all reforms. "It's obvious that the system won't disappear overnight," Gilmore told me. "No abolitionist thinks that will be the case." But she finds First Step, like many state reforms it mimics, not just minor but exclusionary, on account of wording in the bill that will make it even harder for some to get relief. (Those convicted of most higher-level offenses, for example, are ineligible for earned-time credits, a new category created under First Step.) "So many of these proposed remedies don't end up diminishing the system. They regard the system as something that can be fixed by removing and replacing a few elements." For Gilmore, debates over which individuals to let out of prison accept prison as a given. To her, this is not just a moral error but a practical one, if the goal is to actually end mass incarceration. Instead of trying to fix the carceral system, she is focused on policy work to reduce its scope and footprint by stopping new prison construction and closing prisons and jails one facility at a time, with painstaking grass-roots organizing and demands that state funding benefit, rather than punish, vulnerable communities.

"What I love about abolition," the legal scholar and author James

Forman Jr. told me, "and now use in my own thinking — and when I identify myself as an abolitionist, this is what I have in mind — is the idea that you imagine a world without prisons, and then you work to try to build that world." Forman came late, he said, to abolitionist thinking. He was on tour for his 2017 Pulitzer Prize-winning book, "Locking Up Our Own," which documents the history of mass incarceration and the inadvertent roles that black political leaders played, when a woman asked him why he didn't use the word "abolition" in his arguments, which, to her, sounded so abolitionist. The question led Forman to engage seriously with the concept. "I feel like a movement to end mass incarceration and replace it with a system that actually restores and protects communities will never succeed without abolitionists. Because people will make compromises and sacrifices, and they'll lose the vision. They'll start to think things are huge victories, when they're tiny. And so, to me, abolition is essential."

The A.C.L.U.'s Smart Justice campaign, the largest in the organization's history, has been started with a goal of reducing the prison population by 50 percent through local, state and federal initiatives to reform bail, prosecution, sentencing, parole and re-entry. "Incarceration does not work," said the A.C.L.U. campaign director Udi Ofer. The A.C.L.U., he told me, wants to "defund the prison system and reinvest in communities." In our conversation, I found myself wondering if Ofer, and the A.C.L.U., had been influenced by abolitionist thinking and Gilmore. Ofer even seemed to quote Gilmore's mantra that "prisons are catchall solutions to social problems." When I asked him, Ofer said, "There's no question. She's made tremendous contributions, even just in helping to bring about a conversation on what this work really is, and the constant struggle not to replace one oppressive system with another."

Of the A.C.L.U.'s objectives, Gilmore is both hopeful and cautious. "I look forward to seeing how they revise their approach from the exclusionary First Step Act," she told me, "and to seeing how their ambitions, working in multiple jurisdictions, play out." In the last decade, prison populations nationally have shrunk by only 7 percent, and according to the Vera Institute of Justice, 40 percent of this reduction can be attributed to California, which in 2011 was mandated by the Supreme Court to solve overcrowding. Ofer conceded that the greatest challenge is to stop sorting who receives relief based on a divide between violent and nonviolent offenses. "To genuinely end mass incarceration in America, we have to transform how the justice system responds to *all* offenses," Ofer said. "Politically, this is a hard conversation. But morally, it's clear what the direction must be: dismantling the system."

CRITICS HAVE BEEN asking whether prisons themselves were the best solutions to social problems since the birth of the penitentiary system. In 1902, the famous trial lawyer Clarence Darrow told men held in Chicago's Cook County Jail: "There should be no jails. They do not accomplish what they pretend to accomplish." By the late 1960s and early 1970s, an abolition movement had gained traction among a diverse range of people, including scholars, policymakers (even centrist ones), legislators and religious leaders in the United States. In Scandinavia, a prison-abolition movement led to, if not the eradication of prisons, a shift to "open prisons" that emphasize reintegrating people into society and have had very low recidivism rates. After the 1971 uprising at the Attica Correctional Facility outside Buffalo, N.Y., resulting in the deaths of 43 people, there was growing sentiment in the United States that drastic changes were needed. In 1976, a Quaker prison minister named Fay Honey Knopp and a group of activists published the booklet "Instead of Prisons: A Handbook for Abolitionists," which outlined three main goals: to establish a moratorium on all new prison building, to decarcerate those currently in prison and to "excarcerate" — i.e., move away from criminalization and from the use of incarceration altogether. The path that abolitionists called for to achieve these goals seemed strikingly similar to the original (if ultimately failed) goals of the Great Society and "war on crime" laid out by Lyndon B. Johnson in the mid to late 1960s: to generate millions of new jobs, combat employment discrimination, desegregate schools, broaden the social safety net and build new housing. But the ravaging impact of deindustrialization on urban communities had already begun, and it was addressed not with vast social programs but with new and harsh forms of criminalization.

By the late 1990s, as prisons and prison populations expanded significantly, a new call emerged to try to stop states from building more prisons, centered in California and led by, among others, Gilmore and Angela Davis, with the formation of groups like the California Prison Moratorium Project, which Gilmore helped found. In 1998, Davis and Gilmore, along with a group of people in the Bay Area, founded Critical Resistance, a national anti-prison organization that made abolition its central tenet — a goal dismissed by many as utopian and naïve. Five years later, Californians United for a Responsible Budget (CURB), of which Gilmore is a board member, was formed to fight jail and prison construction. CURB quickly rose to prominence for its successful campaigns, which, at last count, have prevented over 140,000 new jail and prison beds (in a state where 200,000 are currently held in prisons and jails). CURB just recently succeeded in halting construction of a huge new women's jail in Los Angeles County, in coordination with several local groups.

Each of the many campaigns Gilmore worked on over the years was built from a different coalition of people who could be negatively affected by a new jail or prison. Her strategy was not to simply fight prisons directly and hope others joined in but rather to seek out groups that were already mobilized. Whether environmentalists who could be made to realize that a new prison would harm biodiversity, or local community members worried about a prison's impact on the water table or undeliverable promises of local employment, "whatever is already there, in terms of people who are organized, that is how to direct the work," Gilmore told me. "You have to talk to people and see what they want." In 2004, for example, there was a measure on the Los Angeles County ballot to hire 5,000 new police officers and deputy sheriffs and to start expanding the city's jail. Gilmore helped organize a campaign in South Central and East Los Angeles, meeting and talking to people, getting them to ask questions and to express their needs. Did the needs of neighborhood residents coincide with the needs of the Los Angeles County Sheriff's and Police Departments? Did they want more police officers in their communities? The answer was no. The measure failed. "It was plodding work — organizing, and organizing, and organizing — but we won. We beat them back."

When the state wanted to build what it was calling new "gender-responsive" prisons, abolitionists organized with people in California women's prisons. The organization Justice Now circulated a petition that 3,300 incarcerated people signed, to protest the new facilities intended to house them. A list of the incarcerated signatories — a 25-foot scroll — was presented at the State Capitol, to audible gasps from the Senate Budget Subcommittee on Prisons. The proposal by the state's Gender Responsive Strategies Commission was defeated. "It's not that everybody who was organized on these campaigns was themselves an abolitionist," Gilmore told me, "but instead that abolitionists engaged in a certain kind of organizing that made all different kinds of people, in all different kinds of situations, decide for themselves that it was not a good idea to have another prison."

BY THE TIME Gilmore began graduate studies at Rutgers University, in 1994 at the age of 43, she was a seasoned activist who had benefited from an extensive informal education with scholars like Cedric Robinson, Barbara Smith and Mike Davis, the author of "City of Quartz," who popularized the term "prison-industrial complex." Gilmore originally thought to pursue a Ph.D. in planning at Rutgers, which seemed the closest to what she wanted to do: parse social problems in relation to the world we've built. Then she encountered the work of the influential Marxist geographer Neil Smith and quickly decided to mail her application to the geography department instead. Geography, she discovered, allowed her to examine urban-rural connections and to think broadly about how life is organized into competing and cooperating systems.

Gilmore received her Ph.D. four years later and was hired the next year as an assistant professor at Berkeley. She wanted to call the first course she taught there "Carceral Geography." The head of the department disapproved. "Can't you call it 'Race and Crime'?" he asked. She replied that her course was not about race and crime. (The department head has a different recollection.) She got her way and has been developing the concept of carceral geography ever since, a category of scholarship she more or less single-handedly invented, which examines the complex interrelationships among landscape, natural resources, political economy, infrastructure and the policing, jailing, caging and controlling of populations. In the years since, Gilmore has shaped the thinking of many geographers, as well as generations of graduate students and activists.

I saw her ability to situate the problem of prison in a much larger political and economic landscape when Davis and Gilmore engaged in a conversation moderated by Beth Richie, a law and African-American studies professor at the University of Illinois at Chicago, in a large church in the city, the three of them — black, radical, feminist intellectuals — seated in huge and ornate bishops' chairs. The event, organized by Critical Resistance, was crowded with South Side organizers, the youngest of whom were invited onstage to offer tributes to Davis, the most famous person in the room. It was all feel-good vibes, and then Davis turned to Gilmore and brought up the topic of private prisons. The tone in the room grew tense.

By now it has become almost conventional wisdom to think that private prisons are the "real" problem with mass incarceration. But anyone seriously engaged with the subject knows that this is not the case. Even a cursory glance at numbers proves it: Ninety-two percent of people locked inside American prisons are held in publicly run, publicly funded facilities, and 99 percent of those in jail are in public jails. Every private prison could close tomorrow, and not a single person would go home. But the ideas that private prisons are the culprit, and that profit is the motive behind all prisons, have a firm grip on the popular imagination. (Incidentally, it isn't just liberals who focus their outrage on private prisons; as Gilmore points out, so do law-enforcement agencies and guards' unions, for whom private prisons draw off resources they want for themselves.)

Davis noted the "mistake," as she put it, in the film "13th," by Ava DuVernay, in sending a message that the main struggle should be against private prisons. But, she said to Gilmore, she saw the popular emphasis on privatization as useful in demonstrating the ways in which prisons are part of the global capitalist system.

Gilmore replied to her longtime comrade that private prisons are not driving mass incarceration. "They are parasites on it. Which doesn't make them good. Which doesn't make them not culpable for the things of which they are culpable. They are parasites." And then she began a sermon on the difference between the profit motive for a company and how public institutions are funded and run. In her fluency on these subjects, a certain gulf opened between the two women. If Davis's charisma could be described as unflappable eloquence, Gilmore's derives from a fierce and precise analysis, an intolerance of vagaries, and it was Gilmore who commanded the room.

Government agencies don't make profits; instead, they need revenue. State agencies must compete for this revenue, Gilmore explained. Under austerity, the social-welfare function shrinks; the agencies that receive the money are the police, firefighters and corrections. So other agencies start to copy what the police do: The education department, for instance, learns that it can receive money for metal detectors much more easily than it can for other kinds of facility upgrades. And prisons can access funds that traditionally went elsewhere — for example, money goes to county jails and state prisons for "mental health services" rather than into public health generally. "If you follow the money, you don't have to find the company that's profiting," Gilmore explained to me later. "You can find all the people who are dependent on wages paid out by the Department of Corrections. The most powerful lobby group in California are the guards. It's a single trade, with one employer, and it couldn't be easier for them to organize. They can elect everyone from D.A.s up to the governor. They gave Gray Davis a couple million dollars, and he gave them a prison."

The explicit function of prison is to separate people from society, and this costs money. Fifteen and a half billion dollars of the proposed budget for the coming year will go to corrections, and 40 percent of that goes to staff salaries alone, not including benefits and generous pensions. This is state-subsidized employment, not a profit venture.

Between 1982 and 2000, California built 23 new prisons and, Gilmore found, increased the state's prison population by 500 percent. If prison scholars tend to focus on one angle or another of incarceration trends, Gilmore provides the most structurally comprehensive explanations, using California as a case study. In her 2007 book, "Golden Gulag," she draws upon her vast knowledge of political economy and geography to put together a portrait of significant historical change and the drive to embark upon what, as two California state analysts called it, "the largest prison building project in the history of the world." Were prisons a response to rising crime? As Gilmore writes, "Crime went up; crime went down; we cracked down." This sequence, and how crime rates are measured, have been heavily debated, but if this noncausal order is really the case, what was going on? Gilmore outlines four categories of "surplus" to explain the prison-building boom. There was "surplus land," because farmers didn't have enough water to irrigate crops, and economic stagnation meant the land was no longer as valuable. As the California government faced lean years, it was left with what she calls "surplus state capacity" — government agencies that had lost their political mandate to use funding and expertise for social welfare benefits (like schools, housing and hospitals). In the wake of this austerity, investors specializing in public finance found themselves with no market for projects like schools and housing and instead used this "surplus capital" to make a market in prison bonds. And finally, there was "surplus labor," resulting from a population of people who, whether from deindustrialized urban centers or languishing rural areas, had been excluded from the economy — in other words, the people from which prison populations nationwide are drawn.

Prisons are not a result of a desire by "bad" people, Gilmore says, to lock up poor people and people of color. "The state did not wake up one morning and say, 'Let's be mean to black people.' All these other things had to happen that made it turn out like this. It didn't have to turn out like this." Her narrative involves a broad array of players and facts, some direct, some indirect, some coordinated, many not: for instance, farmers who leased or sold land to the state for the building of prisons; the very powerful correctional officers' union, state policy-makers, city governments, cycles of drought, economic crisis and huge deindustrialized urban centers; and the lives and fates of the descendants of those who migrated to Southern California for factory work during World War II and after. Her fundamental point is that prison was not inevitable — not for individuals and not for California. But the more prisons the state built, the better the state became at filling them, even despite falling crime rates.

"Golden Gulag" has seminal status among Gilmore's academic peers and activist network, and also more widely — Jay-Z praised it in Time magazine — but certain sections of the book can be intimidatingly technical. Even Gilmore suspects that some who name-check it haven't actually sat down to read it. "The situation — causes, effects — are complicated," she told me, "and people want something that's easy." And yet when Gilmore interacts with people, whether one on one or with an audience, she is direct and accessible. She has a warm and effusive demeanor and is quick to laugh with people and bond with them. She speaks plainly and yet refuses to oversimplify. She gets people thinking about interconnections among larger structures that lead to the creation of prisons, and also interconnections among groups of people that might work together to resist the building of prisons — like environmental activists and teachers' unions.

It is in this manner that she organized in 1999 with both farmworkers and farmers ("in capitalist terms, natural antagonists," as she pointed out to me) to stop a proposed prison in Tulare County, and successfully persuaded the California State Employees Association (CSEA) — then a union of more than 80,000 members — to support a campaign to oppose a new prison in Delano. "The guards could not believe that these public-service employees would go up against other public-service employees," she told me. "Even we were surprised." CSEA came to the understanding, as Gilmore recalls, that a guard is a state worker who has to have a prison to have a job, while state-employed locksmiths, secretaries, janitors and so forth didn't need to work in prisons but might have to, if the guards' union got all the resources.

Despite a lawsuit initiated by a coalition of legal and human rights groups, including Critical Resistance, and environmental concerns raised by a state senator, the prison in Delano did eventually open in 2005, but according to Gilmore it took many years longer than it would have without abolitionists' campaigning against it. "It got to the point where in Sacramento, they were saying, 'Just let us build this one, and we won't build any more.' That's how they talked to us, because they got so tired of us. 'Just let us do this, this will be our last one.' Before the ribbon cutting, the secretary of corrections said, 'This is probably the last prison we're going to open in this state.' He did not say 'because the abolitionists got in our way,' or 'the abolitionists organized all these people that got in our way,' but the implication was there."

"TO UNDERSTAND Ruthie, you have to understand where she came from, what her family was like," Mike Davis told me. Gilmore was born in 1950 and grew up in New Haven, Conn., with three brothers in a household that she calls "decidedly Afro-Saxon," quoting the term that one of her mentors, the political theorist Cedric Robinson, used to describe the family of W.E.B. Du Bois. "Puritan determination was our thing," she told me. "I could not fail, because everything I did was for black people." Gilmore's family attended what was then Dixwell Avenue Congregational Church, which was heavily involved in the civil rights movement. "There was an ethos in my little church," she said. "Everyone needs to learn as much as they can." They had black-history lessons in Sunday school, where they were encouraged to wonder and ask questions. "If you made a claim, the rule was, you had to be able to tell someone how you knew it."

As a child, Gilmore secretly wanted to be a preacher. On Sundays, in the pew, she would imagine herself in the pulpit in preacher's robes. "Which is strange because I could barely open my mouth with strangers. So why I could imagine myself scolding and encouraging the masses, I don't know."

Gilmore's father, Courtland Seymour Wilson, a tool-and-die maker for the firearm manufacturer Winchester, played a central role in organizing Winchester's machinists. The only time in her childhood that white people came to the house was for labor meetings. She would sit on the stairs and listen to the men, who smoked and argued late into the night. As they left, she would peek through a window to watch them leave. "There was always a car outside that people had not gotten out of. It left when the others left." When she learned about Pinkertons, who spied on mineworkers, Gilmore realized the men who parked outside her house were company spies, the equivalent of Pinkertons.

Gilmore's father had inherited a tradition of labor organizing from his own father, a janitor at Yale who helped to organize the first blue-collar workers' union at the university. Eventually Gilmore's father also ended up employed by Yale, where he worked to desegregate its medical school. "He was without question the leader of the civil rights struggle in New Haven," Davis told me.

While Gilmore's father was not college-educated, he was intellectually driven and encouraged Gilmore, a daddy's girl who showed much academic promise. In 1960, a local private school decided to desegregate before it was legally forced to, and sent letters to respected black churches asking about girls who might be "appropriate." Gilmore took the school's entrance exam, which was the same test it gave white girls, and passed. ("It was an easy exam. Like, for [expletive]'s sake, what was all the fuss?") Gilmore was the school's first and, for much of her time there, only black student, and one of a small number of working-class students. She was miserable, but she learned a lot.

In 1968, she enrolled at Swarthmore College, where she got involved in campus politics. It was the year of occupations. She and a group of other black students, among them Angela Davis's younger sister, Fania, wanted to persuade the administration to enroll more black students, and Davis, on a visit to Swarthmore, gave the students advice. "She seemed so amazingly mature and knowledgeable to me," Gilmore said. "I was 19, and she was 24. She had the Alabama style, talked slowly and deliberately, wore a miniskirt." Davis told them: "Figure out what you want, and stick with it. Make a demand."

In January, Gilmore, Fania and a handful of other black students took over the admissions office. Gilmore invited her parents to come down from New Haven and offer political guidance. It was decided that Gilmore and her father, representing the group, would approach Swarthmore's president, Courtney Smith. When they found him, Gilmore, who was raised with formal manners, said, "President Smith, I'd like to introduce you to my father." Smith turned his back and walked away. Gilmore was outraged, but her father was casual. "He knew how to keep his eyes on the prize. What's it about? It's definitely not about *that*."

Gilmore's parents left, and the occupation continued. Eight days into the occupation, Smith had a heart attack at 52 and died at his desk. White students spread a rumor that Gilmore and her cohort were in the president's office, yelling at him when he died (in reality, they were nowhere near his office), and there were rumors that they had threatened to get revenge.

At the time, Swarthmore, just like Yale, had a large number of black employees who performed the necessary if less visible jobs around campus, and these people, it turned out, had been observing events from a distance. "They decided to save us," Gilmore told me. "Cars pulled into the circular drive, and these black men got out and stood looking up at us, in the windows. We left with them. It all seemed magical to me. It was ontology put into action, that made it possible for folks to pull up in these cars and silently wait to rescue us, and we knew to be rescued."

The men drove them to a house where they bedded down for the night. The next morning, some people went out for supplies and returned with food and a copy of that morning's paper. In the paper was a picture of Gilmore's cousin, John Huggins. He had served in Vietnam and been radicalized upon his return, becoming a founding member of the Southern California chapter of the Black Panthers. Now he and another Panther, Bunchy Carter, had been murdered on the U.C.L.A. campus by a rival political group.

Her cousin's murder was a personal devastation, if also a symptom of the politics of the time (as later came to light, the F.B.I. had infiltrated these organizations, in order to create the divisions that most likely contributed to this fatal encounter). Gilmore left Swarthmore and moved home. Later that year, she enrolled at Yale and got deeply involved with her studies.

"Every year I had one teacher who was really good to me, interested in what I thought about and wrote," she said. One of them was George Steiner. Another was the film and drama critic Stanley Kauffmann. Gilmore graduated with a degree in drama before vagabonding across the country. She ended up in Southern California, where she met her husband, Craig Gilmore, and embarked on organizing work they've participated in together since 1976.

GILMORE HAS COME to understand that there are certain narratives people cling to that are not only false but that allow for policy positions aimed at minor or misdirected — rather than fundamental and meaningful — reforms. Gilmore takes apart these narratives: that a significant number of people are in prison for nonviolent drug convictions; that prison is a modified continuation of slavery, and, by extension, that most everyone in prison is black; and, as she explained in Chicago, that corporate profit motive is the primary engine of incarceration.

For Gilmore, and for a growing number of scholars and activists, the idea that prisons are filled with nonviolent offenders is particularly problematic. Less than one in five nationally are in prisons or jail for drug offenses, but this notion proliferated in the wake of the overwhelming popularity of Michelle Alexander's "The New Jim Crow," which focuses on the devastating effects of the war on drugs, cases that are primarily handled by the (relatively small) federal prison system. It's easy to feel outrage about draconian laws that punish nonviolent drug offenders, and about racial bias, each of which Alexander catalogs in a riveting and persuasive manner. But a majority of people in state and federal prisons have been convicted of what are defined as violent offenses, which can include everything from possession of a gun to murder. This statistical reality can be uncomfortable for some people, but instead of grappling with it, many focus on the "relatively innocent," as Gilmore calls them, the addicts or the falsely accused — never mind that they can only ever represent a small percentage of those in prison. When I asked Michelle Alexander about this, she responded: "I think the failure of some academics like myself to squarely respond to the question of violence in our work has created a situation in which it almost seems like we're approving of mass incarceration for violent people. Those of us who are committed to ending the system of mass criminalization have to begin talking more about violence. Not only the harm it causes, but the fact that building more cages will never solve it."

But in the United States, it's difficult for people to talk about prison without assuming there is a population that must stay there. "When people are looking for the relative innocence line," Gilmore told me, "in order to show how sad it is that the relatively innocent are being subjected to the forces of state-organized violence as though they were criminals, they are missing something that they could see. It isn't that hard. They could be asking whether people who have been criminalized should be subjected to the forces of organized violence. They could ask if we need organized violence."

Another widely held misconception Gilmore points to is that prison is majority black. Not only is it a false and harmful stereotype to over-associate black people with prison, she argues, but by not acknowledging racial demographics and how they shift from one state to another, and over time, the scope and crisis of mass incarceration can't be fully comprehended. In terms of racial demographics, black people are the population most affected by mass incarceration — roughly 33 percent of those in prison are black, while only 12 percent of the United States population is — but Latinos still make up 23 percent of the prison population and white people 30 percent, according to the Bureau of Justice Statistics. (Gilmore has heard people argue that drug laws will change because the opioid epidemic hurts rural whites, a myth that drives her crazy. "People say, 'God knows they're not going to lock up white people,'" she told me, "and it's like, Yes, they *do* lock up white people.") Once you believe prisons are predominately black, it's also easier to believe that prisons are a conspiracy to re-enslave black people — a narrative, Gilmore acknowledges, that offers two crucial truths: that the struggles and suffering of black people are central to the story of mass incarceration, and that prison, like slavery, is a human rights catastrophe. But prison as a modern version of Jim Crow mostly serves to allow people to worry about a population they might otherwise ignore. "The guilty are worthy of being ignored, and yet mass incarceration is so phenomenal that people are trying to find a way to care about those who are guilty of crimes. So, in order to care about them, they have to have some category to which they become worthy of worry. And the category is slavery."

A person who eventually either steals something or assaults someone goes to prison, where he is offered no job training, no redress of his own traumas and issues, no rehabilitation. "The reality of prison, and of black suffering, is just as harrowing as the myth of slave labor," Gilmore says. "Why do we need that misconception to see the horror of it?" Slaves were compelled to work in order to make profits for plantation owners. The business of slavery was cotton, sugar and rice. Prison, Gilmore notes, is a government institution. It is not a business and does not function on a profit motive. This may seem technical, but the technical distinction matters, because you can't resist prisons by arguing against slavery if prisons don't engage in slavery. The activist and researcher James Kilgore, himself formerly incarcerated, has said, "The overwhelming problem for people inside prison is not that their labor is super exploited; it's that they're being warehoused with very little to do and not being given any kind of programs or resources that enable them to succeed once they do get out of prison."

The National Employment Law Project estimates that about 70 million people have a record of arrest or conviction, which often makes employment difficult. Many end up in the informal economy, which has been absorbing a huge share of labor over the last 20 years. "Gardener, home health care, sweatshops, you name it," Gilmore told me. "These people have a place in the economy, but they have no control over that place." She continued: "The key point here, about half of the work force, is to think not only about the enormity of the problem, but the enormity of the possibilities! That so many people could benefit from being organized into solid formations, could make certain kinds of demands, on the people who pay their wages, on the communities where they live. On the schools their children go to. This is part of what abolitionist thinking should lead us to."

"Abolition," as a word, is an intentional echo of the movement to abolish slavery. "This work will take generations, and I'm not going to be alive to see the changes," the activist Mariame Kaba told me. "Similarly I know that our ancestors, who were slaves, could not have imagined my life." And as Kaba and Davis and Richie and Gilmore all told me, unsolicited and in almost identical phrasing, it is not serendipity that the movement of prison abolition is being led by black women. Davis and Richie each used the term "abolition feminism." "Historically, black feminists have had visions to change the structure of society in ways that would benefit not just black women but everyone," Davis said. She also talked about Du Bois and the lessons drawn from his conception of what was needed: not merely a lack of slavery but a new society, utterly transformed. "I think the fact that so many people now do call themselves prison abolitionists," Michelle Alexander told me, "is a testament to the fact that an enormous amount of work has been done, in academic circles and in grass-root circles. Still, if you just say 'prison abolition' on CNN, you're going to have a lot of people shaking their heads. But Ruthie has always been very clear that prison abolition is not just about closing prisons. It's a theory of change."

When Gilmore encounters an audience that is hostile to prison abolition, an audience that supposes she's naïvely suggesting that those in prison are there for smoking weed, and wants to tell her who's really locked up, what terrible things they've done, she tells them she's had a loved one murdered and isn't there to talk about people who smoke weed. But as she acknowledged to me, "Part of the whole story that can't be denied is that people are tired of harm, they are tired of grief and they are tired of anxiety." She described to me conversations she'd had with people who are glad their abusive husband or father has been removed from their home, and would not want it any other way. Of her own encounter with murder, she's more philosophical, even if the loss still seems raw.

"I had this heart-to-heart with my aunt, the mother of my murdered cousin, John. On the surface, we were talking about something else, but we were really talking about him. I said, 'Forgive and forget.' And she replied, 'Forgive, but *never* forget.' She was right: The conditions under which the atrocity occurred must change, so that they can't occur again."

For Gilmore, to "never forget" means you don't solve a problem with state violence or with personal violence. Instead, you change the conditions under which violence prevailed. Among liberals, a kind of quasi-Christian idea about empathy circulates, the idea that we have to find a way to care about the people who've done bad. To Gilmore this is unconvincing. When she encountered the kids in Fresno who hassled her about prison abolition, she did not ask them to empathize with the people who might hurt them, or had. She instead asked them why, as individuals, and as a society, we believe that the way to solve a problem is by "killing it." She was asking if punishment is logical, and if it works. She let the kids find their own way to answer.

RACHEL KUSHNER is a writer in Los Angeles. Her most recent novel is "The Mars Room." She last wrote for the magazine about a Palestinian refugee camp.

CHAPTER 6

Tough Transitions and Institutional Resistance

The criminal justice system is currently in the midst of transformation. Prison populations have decreased, facilities have closed, and task forces have been appointed to improve the relationship between police and communities. However, the character of that change itself is unsettled and under fierce dispute, between reformists, radicals and those who don't want the current system to change. The articles in this chapter reveal these challenges, allowing us to critically assess these three points of view.

In the Bronx, New Life for an Old Prison

OPINION | BY JESSE WEGMAN | FEB. 2, 2015

THE SEVEN-STORY, faded-brick building at 1511 Fulton Avenue — across from Crotona Park in the Claremont section of the Bronx — has no distinct personality, which may help explain why it has been reincarnated so many times over the past century.

It began life in 1907 as an Episcopal church house. By the 1920s, the area was heavily Jewish, and the building became a Young Men's Hebrew Association, with a synagogue on the ground floor. In the 1950s, it was a nursing home. Later it operated as a drug treatment center.

A view from the roof of the Fulton Correctional Facility in the Bronx.

Each time, the building's new use tracked the shifting demographics and needs of New York City.

Today it sits vacant. If local residents think of it at all, they probably remember it not as a house of worship, but for its service of a different sort of penitent: For nearly four decades, it was the Fulton Correctional Facility, a minimum-security prison that housed up to 900 inmates on work release.

The state closed the prison four years ago, one of 13 facilities the administration of Gov. Andrew Cuomo has shut down in the wake of a major drop in the state's inmate population, from nearly 73,000 in 1999 to 54,000 in 2012.

But last week the building at 1511 Fulton began its latest transformation, this time into a community re-entry center that will provide temporary housing and job training to New Yorkers returning from prison.

On Jan. 28, the city signed over the building's deed to the Osborne Association, an 82-year-old prison reform group that will operate the center after extensive renovations, thanks mainly to a $6 million grant from a state fund established for communities where prisons have closed.

Elizabeth Gaynes, Osborne's executive director, has been the driving force behind the re-entry center. At a ceremonial handover of the building's keys on Thursday, she thanked state officials for the opportunity. New York's corrections department, Ms. Gaynes said, has "generally behaved like proud parents who are marrying off their child to someone of a different religion."

It will take some work to make 1511 Fulton look like a place that people aren't forced at gunpoint to live in. Gray cinderblock walls, low ceilings and dim, scuffed hallways ring the floors. The cells — some no more than eight feet square — are bare but for barred, dirt-caked windows and metal toilets bolted to the walls.

As the country's 40-year incarceration boom has leveled off, states have struggled with what to do with abandoned prisons. Some have been converted into hotels, others into homeless shelters, a cemetery, a summer camp and a movie studio. But 1511 Fulton is the first to become a multipurpose re-entry center, Ms. Gaynes said.

In addition to initial housing and job assistance for 60 to 70 former inmates, the center plans to host a range of businesses to help replace jobs lost when the prison shut its doors — including catering and furniture-refurbishing companies and, on the roof, an apiary.

That can only help in the Bronx, which has the highest unemployment rate in the state. The district that includes Fulton also has one of the highest concentrations of public housing in New York City. Many inmates have family in that housing, but they cannot move there, because New York law almost always prevents people with a criminal record from living in public housing.

On the other hand, a familiarity with former prisoners may have made it easier to win community acceptance of the center. Unlike in Brooklyn, where a new parole center in the Gowanus neighborhood has generated heated opposition, there was virtually none to the

Fulton center proposal. "It's what I love about the Bronx," Ms. Gaynes said in an interview. "They don't act like we're importing Martians. They understand that if people get the right assistance, they can be assets to the community."

After the key ceremony, Stanley Richards stood hunched by a wall in a suit and tie, remembering his days as an involuntary resident of 1511 Fulton.

"You see I'm sweating?" Mr. Richards said. "My gut is going up and down. When I walked in that door, I remembered when I first walked in that door, not knowing if I was coming back out."

Following a robbery conviction, he served four and a half years at an upstate prison before being transferred to Fulton's work-release program in 1991. He found a $5-an-hour job as a telemarketer, selling timeshares on Fire Island. The office was in Manhattan, so he left the prison every morning at seven and was due back by six. He slept in a cell with seven other inmates.

Now 54, Mr. Richards is married with four children, and is a senior vice president at the Fortune Society, which helps former prisoners adapt to the outside world. But it was a close call: Mr. Richards nearly missed out on the work-release program, which was decimated by the Pataki administration after his release. Today it operates at less than 10 percent of its peak in the early 1990s. Mr. Richards said that for him, as for the thousands of prisoners returning each year, success ultimately depends on having a job and a place to live.

"If they don't think anything's possible for them, they're going to act like that," he said. "If they see potential, they're going to act like that. So this opening is a step in helping people realize you can have a second chance."

JESSE WEGMAN joined the Times editorial board in 2013. He was previously a senior editor at The Daily Beast and Newsweek, a legal news editor at Reuters, and the managing editor of The New York Observer.

Rahm Emanuel Unveils Changes for Chicago Police but Ignores Much of Panel's Advice

BY MITCH SMITH | APRIL 21, 2016

CHICAGO — Mayor Rahm Emanuel called on Thursday for better training, speedier misconduct investigations and other immediate changes for the troubled Chicago Police Department. His plan came in response to a scathing report published last week that blamed racism and a broken discipline process for the frayed trust between officers and many residents, validating complaints made for years by African-Americans in the city.

But Mr. Emanuel's plan did not address about 70 percent of the recommendations from the Police Accountability Task Force, which he appointed in December after demonstrators demanded his resignation. He said in a statement on Thursday that city officials would release progress reports as more changes took effect.

Lori Lightfoot, the chairwoman of the task force, said that it was "important that the mayor has taken initiative" to start making changes, but that all of the recommendations were meant to eventually be adopted.

Thursday's announcement came at a time of continuing turmoil for the Police Department. The Justice Department is reviewing its practices, the City Council confirmed a new police superintendent last week, and violent crime has spiked.

Here are findings by the task force and changes announced by Mr. Emanuel.

COMMUNITY RELATIONS

TASK FORCE'S FINDING *"The community's lack of trust in C.P.D. is justified. There is substantial evidence that people of color — particularly African-Americans — have had disproportionately negative experiences with the police over an extended period of time."*

Protesters marched repeatedly after the release in November of video showing a white police officer firing 16 shots into a black teenager, Laquan McDonald.

CITY'S PLAN Eddie Johnson, the new police superintendent, has held "bridge meetings" with residents in recent days and has pledged to continue those. The Chicago police have also started using "restorative justice" to connect officers with young people of different cultures to discuss race, bias and other issues. "Trust is at the heart of good policing, safe communities, and is the central challenge facing Chicago today," Mr. Johnson said in the mayor's statement. "These reforms are a down payment on restoring that trust."

MENTAL HEALTH

TASK FORCE'S FINDING *"There have increasingly been situations in which police response to calls involving persons experiencing mental health crises ended with devastating results."*

Philip Coleman, a 38-year-old college graduate, died at a hospital in 2012 after being arrested, shocked by a Taser and dragged from his cell in handcuffs while undergoing what his family has described as a mental health crisis. This month, the City Council approved a $4.95 million settlement in his case.

CITY'S PLAN More officers will have crisis-intervention training to respond to mentally ill people, as the task force recommended. Dispatchers and 911 operators will be trained in properly dispatching officers to scenes where mental illness is suspected.

Alexa James, a licensed clinical social worker who served on the task force, said that she was encouraged by Thursday's announcement and that "the more tools officers have to support anybody in crisis, the better." But Ms. James, the executive director of the National Alliance on Mental Illness, said she hoped that the mayor would soon create a response unit, suggested by the task force, that would work with community groups and expand and coordinate the Police Department's training.

JOSHUA LOTT FOR THE NEW YORK TIMES

Mayor Rahm Emanuel last week during a Chicago City Council meeting where Eddie Johnson was confirmed as the city's police superintendent.

POLICE MISCONDUCT

TASK FORCE'S FINDING *"Statistics give real credibility to the widespread perception that there is a deeply entrenched code of silence supported not just by individual officers, but by the very institution itself."*

The City Council agreed last year to pay $5.5 million to victims of Jon Burge, a former police commander who tortured suspects and coerced confessions in the 1970s and '80s. Some men who said they had been wrongfully convicted spent years in prison before the city publicly acknowledged the abuses and agreed to pay reparations.

CITY'S PLAN Mr. Emanuel called for an early intervention system to identify and help problem officers, a hotline for officers to report colleagues who are breaking the rules, and a set of fixed penalties for misconduct.

But the mayor largely steered clear of issues the task force had raised about police union contracts. The task force found that some provisions in those contracts provided too much protection to officers who committed misconduct. Dean Angelo Sr., the president of the union that represents rank-and-file officers, said Thursday that the report was "not fair at all" and that he did not understand why Mr. Emanuel was carrying out task force recommendations while the Justice Department was still investigating. Mr. Angelo said that his members were frustrated and angry with what he considered "finger-pointing," and that claims that officers were racist were especially unfair.

POLICE SHOOTING INVESTIGATIONS

TASK FORCE'S FINDING *Explaining why the Independent Police Review Authority, which investigates police shootings and severe misconduct, should be replaced: "Cases go uninvestigated, the agency lacks resources, and I.P.R.A.'s findings raise troubling concerns about whether it is biased in favor of police officers."*

A former investigator for the police review authority, Lorenzo Davis, said he had been overruled and fired when he wanted to fault officers in some shootings. In one case, he said, he sought to find wrongdoing in the 2013 shooting death of Cedrick Chatman, who was running away from officers and carrying an iPhone box. The police said they had mistaken the box for a gun.

CITY'S PLAN Mr. Emanuel did not immediately call for doing away with the review authority, but city officials indicated willingness to consider "options for structural reform." Mr. Emanuel endorsed plans to audit past investigations, increase outreach, and work on a system to release video and other evidence after police shootings.

Ms. Lightfoot, the task force's chairwoman, said she hoped a new agency would eventually be created to take over those investigations. "People are expecting that there are going to be some dramatic changes done and that a new organization is going to be stood up," she said. "That hasn't been addressed, but we're a week into this."

For Real Community Policing, Let Officers Do Their Jobs

OPINION | BY PATRICK J. LYNCH | OCT. 27, 2016

ALL POLICING SHOULD BE community policing. Police officers and residents work together every day, because it's the only way to keep the streets safe. Over the past 30 years, though, whenever there has been a need to heal a rift between the police and the public, this basic principle has gotten watchword status.

We face such a rift today, particularly in New York City's African-American and Hispanic communities, largely because of Police Department policies that inhibit true community policing and set harmful quotas for arrests and other police activities, like "stop, question and frisk."

Police officers have recognized for decades that the department was driving a wedge between officers and the people we serve by making our jobs dependent on meeting these mandates — reducing public safety to a numbers game. As far back as 2004, the Patrolmen's Benevolent Association warned that quotas were harming residents and police officers alike, and we filed grievances and fought for expanded state anti-quota legislation to stop it.

Unfortunately, our elected leaders and the courts have too often ignored these failed management policies, focusing instead on saddling police officers on the street with additional burdens and scrutiny. In doing so, they have advanced the false narrative that New York City police officers are, as a group, bad actors motivated by personal racial prejudice. This narrative has made our jobs far more difficult, and has further damaged the relationship with the New Yorkers we serve.

Now the city is once again calling for community policing as a means of repairing the damage, and once again some officers on the street and community members are skeptical. We have seen similar strategies, such as the Community Patrol Officer Program from the

1980s, tried out and eventually abandoned. In order for the current iteration of community policing to succeed, it must be given the proper staffing resources. It must also treat police officers as professionals and allow them the discretion to effectively carry out the strategy in the real world.

But our head count has dropped by approximately 6,000. Many precincts face a serious backlog of radio calls, and officers on patrol are routinely assigned multiple jobs at once. Meanwhile, officers are pulled from local precincts to staff specialized units or to cover special events.

Now, under the current plan for community policing, a handful of neighborhood coordination officers would have dedicated time off their radios to address community policing issues. But if that forces others to double up or keeps them from responding to potentially critical calls, we'll be making things worse and could even prevent the development of strong ties with the community.

The department may want officers at every precinct community council meeting, participating in pickup basketball games, and stopping by local cookouts. But attending these structured activities goes only so far to address what the community needs. What most New Yorkers want from the police are not photo ops for the department's social media channels, but for officers to listen and respond to their concerns when they have them.

Officers want to have those types of conversations. They let us resolve some situations without resorting to enforcement action while also learning who the truly bad actors are. It's not enough for those conversations to happen only at formalized community policing activities.

Unfortunately, like the numerically driven enforcement model, the formal community policing strategy implies that officers cannot be treated as professionals, trusted to exercise proper judgment in any situation without micromanagement. It pressures them to produce documentable "activity," paralyzes them with bureaucratic second-guessing and threatens to turn "community engagement" into just another box to check.

If this approach continues the department will lose smart, highly qualified officers to other police departments that provide competitive wages, respect and fairer treatment. Stronger community relationships require keeping our best police officers and being able to recruit the best. They also mean giving them incentives to remain in roles that work directly with the community, instead of jumping at the first opportunity to get off the street and into a specialized unit.

If city neighborhoods lose these officers and cannot attract new ones of the same caliber, the impact will be significant, especially in the areas that need them most.

New York City police officers don't want to look elsewhere, because the communities we protect are our communities, too. Sixty percent of New York City police officers live in the five boroughs. We want the same as our fellow New Yorkers: safe and livable streets. If we work together, with the tools, support and the right strategy, we will make sure our communities are safer and stronger for years to come.

PATRICK J. LYNCH is the president of the New York City Patrolmen's Benevolent Association.

There's a Wave of New Prosecutors. And They Mean Justice.

OPINION | BY EMILY BAZELON AND MIRIAM KRINSKY | DEC. 11, 2018

These district attorneys should make jail the exception and eliminate cash bail.

IN THE PAST TWO YEARS, a wave of prosecutors promising less incarceration and more fairness have been elected across the country.

Republicans and Democrats are among the reformers, and they're taking over district attorney offices in red and blue states. Five progressive D.A.s have been elected in major cities in Texas, of all surprising places, most recently in Dallas and San Antonio. In Houston, Kim Ogg was elected D.A. two years ago, and in the face of opposition from more than a dozen local judges, she has supported a lawsuit challenging the cash bail system for misdemeanor cases.

Local prosecutors, who handle 95 percent of the criminal cases brought in this country, are well positioned to take reform into their own hands because of their broad discretion over whether and how to prosecute cases and what bail they decide to seek against defendants.

And they're exercising that discretion in new ways.

In Chicago, State Attorney Kim Foxx raised the threshold for felony theft prosecution to reduce the number of shoplifters who go to jail. In Philadelphia, the D.A., Larry Krasner, has instructed his prosecutors to make plea offers for most crimes below the bottom end of Pennsylvania's sentencing guidelines. In Kansas City, Kan., District Attorney Mark Dupree created a unit to scrutinize old cases haunted by questionable police practices despite opposition from local law enforcement. More broadly, many of these new, progressive prosecutors are declining to prosecute low-level marijuana offenses and have stopped asking for bail in most misdemeanor cases.

But they've also encountered tough headwinds. We've seen these new district attorneys in action, and with input from two policy groups, the Justice Collaborative and the Brennan Center for Justice, we've come up with a set of principles and priorities to promote a progressive model of prosecution. There are 21 principles in all that offer D.A.s a blueprint to transform both their own offices and, with a push from advocates on the outside and help from other leaders on the inside, their justice systems. Since laws and practices vary from state to state, some of our recommendations won't suit all jurisdictions. We intend them as a starting point.

Our recommendations begin with the premise that the level of punishment in the United States is neither necessary for public safety nor a pragmatic use of resources. Prosecutors can address this first by routing some low-level offenses out of the criminal justice system at the start. For the cases that remain, they can help make incarceration the exception and diverting people from prison the rule, a principle advanced by the district attorney in Brooklyn, N.Y., Eric Gonzalez. Finally, prosecutors should recognize that lengthy mandatory sentences can be wasteful, since most people age out of the period when they're likely to reoffend, and also don't allow for the human capacity to change.

As prosecutors know, locking people up makes them more prone to committing offenses in the future. They can lose their earning capacity and housing, leaving them worse off, often to the point of desperation. And so the community is often better served by interventions like drug or mental-health treatment, or by restorative justice approaches, in which a person who has caused harm makes amends to the victim. In some cases, the best response is to do nothing.

Achieving results, of course, matters more than making promises. In Brooklyn last Friday, the police arrested Jazmine Headley as she sat on the floor of a food stamp application office because there were no available chairs. The officers yanked her 1-year-old son from her arms, and the D.A.'s office charged her with resisting arrest and other offenses. Although prosecutors agreed to release her without bail, Ms. Headley was held at Rikers Island on a warrant from New Jersey

Lansing Correctional Facility in Lansing, Kan.

for credit card fraud. The arrest was captured on video and outrage ensued. On Tuesday, Mr. Gonzalez said he was "horrified by the violence" on the video, promised to investigate and moved to dismiss the charges. But this arrest shouldn't have happened in the first place, and the response from the D.A. illustrates the back-and-forth between reformers on the outside and an elected prosecutor on the inside.

If making jail the exception in criminal cases sounds revolutionary, it shouldn't. In many cities and counties, misdemeanors make up about 80 percent of the criminal docket. With few exceptions, locking people up for these low-level offenses, and for felonies that don't involve serious violence or injury, is the wrong approach. The states of California, New Jersey and New York have cut the rate of incarceration by about 25 percent even as crime has fallen at a faster pace than it has nationally. In other words, locking up fewer people has correlated with making states safer, not less safe. Nationally, the population of teenagers in detention has also dropped by half alongside a major decline in the crime rate among young people. Internationally, crime is down in developed countries where incarceration always remained relatively low.

To keep people out of jail who don't need to be there, prosecutors have to rethink whether and how they charge defendants in criminal cases. Too often, they bring the maximum charges or stack charges to gain leverage: The bigger the threatened sentence, the more reason defendants have to plead guilty rather than risk everything at trial. A fair process begins with screening cases rigorously as early as possible, so cases supported by only weak evidence can be declined or dismissed. When charges are brought, they should reflect the facts and circumstances of each case, so that they're designed to achieve a just result, not the heaviest possible penalty.

Prosecutors should also treat kids as kids. This means taking science and adolescent brain development into account, and not criminalizing typical adolescent behavior such as fistfights or infractions at school. It also means expunging juvenile records for many of the cases that are resolved or when no new charges are incurred after a few years so young people have a second chance. And it means refraining from trying people under the age of 18 as adults, except in very limited circumstances involving serious violent offenses.

Prosecutors should work to end the devastating impact the justice system has on people because they're poor, by pushing for the elimination of cash bail and fines and fees that people cannot reasonably afford to pay. D.A.s should also push to shrink the number of people — currently about five million — who are under some form of probation or parole. Excessive supervision increases the likelihood that people who are otherwise at low risk of reoffending will end up incarcerated for technical violations like breaking curfew. Some states have shortened supervision periods with no increase in reoffending.

Certain criminal charges and convictions carry especially harsh consequences for immigrants, triggering detention and deportation proceedings. Being jailed before trial also increases the likelihood of being detained and deported by federal immigration officials. Entangling the local justice system in immigration enforcement erodes trust, discouraging immigrants from reporting crime and appearing as witnesses in court. To build trust, prosecutors should consider the immigration consequences of the charges they choose to bring.

Too often, D.A. offices operate like a black box, with crucial decisions about charging and pleas hidden from public view. District attorneys should collect and share data so that the public can hold the system accountable. They should track the outcome of cases by race to flag disparities, findings of prosecutorial and police misconduct, and the number of people who go to jail because they can't pay bail. They should also post data on diversion programs, incarceration rates and what all this costs taxpayers.

In a democracy, people tend to value and uphold the law when they perceive it as fair. As these new D.A.s reimagine the American model of prosecution, they should be pragmatists, focused on the well-being of the communities that elected them. Fairness and safety aren't a trade-off. They complement each other. This new corps of prosecutors can lead the way toward doing more justice with more mercy.

MIRIAM KRINSKY is a former federal prosecutor and the executive director of Fair and Just Prosecution.

EMILY BAZELON is a staff writer at the Magazine and the Truman Capote Fellow for Creative Writing and Law at Yale Law School. She is also a best-selling author and a co-host of the "Slate Political Gabfest," a popular podcast.

How to Close Rikers Island

EDITORIAL | BY THE NEW YORK TIMES | OCT. 13, 2019

Smaller jails, built in different boroughs, are good investments in a safer future.

THE DECLINE IN CRIME over the past three decades in New York City is one of the most striking examples of how a community can change the way it behaves. New Yorkers today are not as violent toward their neighbors as they were in the 1990s and commit fewer crimes. The police make fewer arrests. Prosecutors and judges divert more offenders to alternatives to jail.

The causes for the decline in crime are numerous and hotly contested. But the numbers speak for themselves: In 1990, there were 2,245 murders in the city. The last weekly report from the city lists 249 murders in 2019. That figure doesn't include the four people killed in a shooting in Brooklyn on Saturday. Other types of violent crimes are at historical lows.

As crime has continued to plummet, the number of New Yorkers behind bars has fallen. The population of the city's detainees peaked at more than 21,000 in 1991. This year, the population hovers around 7,100. Between 2013 and 2018, New York City's jail population fell by more than 30 percent. (There would be even fewer people in jail were it not for the hundreds of people held on state technical parole violations who are also sent to city facilities.)

The jailed population is expected to fall even further in the coming years, after Democrats won the first clear majority in the State Legislature in decades in 2018 and approved major criminal justice reforms this year. The reforms take effect in January.

Most people charged with misdemeanors and nonviolent felonies will be released without being required to post cash bail. Judges will have the option of sending those charged with violent felonies to supervised release in some cases. Defense lawyers say that could include, for instance, a minor charged with gun possession, but not gun use. In what many experts view as the most sweeping change, the new law will require prosecutors to disclose evidence to the defense far earlier.

Owing in large part to the reforms, New York City officials project that by 2026 the city's jails will be tasked with housing no more than 3,300 people. With that number in mind, the City Council is expected to vote this month on a plan to close the jail complex at Rikers Island completely by 2026 by sending New Yorkers instead to four jails spread across the five boroughs. The plan would be safer for inmates, safer for guards and more compassionate for the residents of a city that is playing a lead role in ending the era of mass incarceration.

Many see Rikers Island as "synonymous with brutality, incompetence, corruption and neglect," as this page once described it. Fewer know that it was once directly associated with slavery. The island, with more than 400 acres, was named for the family of Richard Riker, a 19th-century court recorder known for zealously sending blacks south into slavery whether or not they were legally free.

Since 1935, the city has used the island to house a sprawling complex of facilities. Over the years, most of the people held on Rikers Island (in addition to three other jails in different boroughs) have been awaiting trial, meaning they haven't been convicted of a crime. Other jail residents were serving short sentences, generally for minor crimes.

The United States incarcerates more of its citizens — both per capita and in absolute terms — than any other country in the world. Some 2.2 million people have been behind bars in the country's prisons and jails this year.

The social and economic cost of the incarceration is high, and it has been disproportionately borne by black and Hispanic communities. Yet research strongly suggests that incarceration had little to do with the decrease in crime, and in fact may have contributed to crime. "We've thrown jail at every problem for so long. We know now that we were wrong," said Scott Hechinger, senior staff attorney and director of policy at Brooklyn Defender Services. "It doesn't enhance safety. It does the opposite, and it costs a fortune."

Rikers continues to be a place of violence and cruelty. In 2010, a 16-year-old African-American by the name of Kalief Browder was accused of stealing a backpack, a crime he said he did not commit, and sent to Rikers. The teenager never received a trial. Yet he remained in jail for three years, including two years in solitary confinement. In 2015, two years after his release, he took his own life, after speaking openly about the trauma the ordeal had caused him.

Mr. Browder's death galvanized the movement to close Rikers Island once and for all. For several years, Mayor Bill de Blasio resisted those calls. In 2017, the mayor — after his re-election and under enormous pressure from community groups — backed a plan to close Rikers.

Though the plan has significant support, it isn't a sure thing. Over the past year, New Yorkers and the officials who represent them have argued over the important details of how to close the complex and what to do with the jails that would replace it.

The plan is supported by the mayor, the City Council speaker, Corey Johnson, and many criminal justice advocates. The new jails would be modern facilities closer to courthouses and communities. Many experts have said building new jails on Rikers Island is impossible, partly because it is close to the runways of La Guardia Airport, limiting the scale of development. They have also said the isolation of the island, combined with a deeply entrenched culture of corruption and violence, is reason enough to close the jails and start anew.

The plan calls for the city to spend more than $8 billion to rebuild three outdated jails, one each in Brooklyn, Queens and Manhattan, to make them safer and more sanitary, and able to accommodate education, mental health and job training services. A fourth jail would be built in the Bronx, which never had a permanent facility, to the same standards. Staten Island would be the only borough without a jail because its residents represent a tiny portion of the city's jail population.

There has been some community opposition to the plan in places where the jails would be built or expanded. Local officials are divided over the plan in the Bronx, where some residents have said they don't want a jail near their homes. At community meetings in the Boerum Hill neighborhood of Brooklyn, many residents have opposed plans to expand the existing jail. Councilman Stephen Levin, who represents the area, has signaled support for rebuilding the Brooklyn jail, but also wants investments in restorative justice programs, mental health, education and health care.

In recent months, some of the fiercest opposition has come from activists and community groups that say the city should close Rikers without building any new jails. They argue that the jail population can be reduced to tiny numbers through more criminal justice reforms, and they have called for the $8 billion-plus estimated cost of the jail plan to be spent on housing, mental health and education. "We are a group of prison industrial complex abolitionists," said Pilar Maschi, a community organizer with No New Jails NYC, a grass-roots coalition that opposes the plan. "Moving a person from one cage to another is not satisfactory."

Ms. Maschi, who was incarcerated on Rikers Island in the 1990s, said the goal wasn't to release all people from jail right now, but rather to reorient the country's focus toward resolving conflicts without using prisons.

Expressing the same interest, Alexandria Ocasio-Cortez, who represents parts of the Bronx and Queens in the House, signaled that she opposed moving jails to individual boroughs. "I know the term 'prison abolition' is breaking some people's brains," Ms. Ocasio-Cortez wrote on Twitter Oct. 7. "We have more than enough room to close many of our prisons and explore just alternatives to incarceration."

There are a limited number of jail beds in New York City outside of Rikers Island. They are also in aging buildings that are dangerous for the jailed and the jailers, and they lack the needed space for programming that makes re-entry to society easier and recidivism less likely. That's the weakness of the effort to close Rikers without building new jails. The reason to build new facilities is for the more humane confinement of people who pose a threat to their communities. We don't know if future generations will seek to jail more New Yorkers or fewer. But infrastructure construction can both enable policy flexibility or lock in past policy preferences. The current plan to close Rikers and build modern facilities gets the balance right.

Having too few beds could lead to overcrowding if a future administration returned to policies that rely on more incarceration. Consider the Vernon C. Bain Center, a, 625-foot barge in the East River, which serves as a five-story, Dickensian floating jail for around 800 people every night. It was a temporary solution in 1992 to overcrowding in an era of mass incarceration. The Bain Center will also be shut if the Council approves the plan.

Another constituency has stubbornly argued against closing Rikers altogether. Those naysayers have included people like former Police Commissioner William Bratton. "What you have is a lot of, unfortunately in many instances, very dangerous people," he said in 2016. "You now want to take them off an island, away from everybody, and put them into neighborhoods?"

Actually, yes. Locating modern facilities in the community is the best solution for those who are jailed and the neighborhoods they call home. Jails are not prisons, facilities built to isolate the most violent members of society for decades or lifetimes. Nearly everyone who is jailed will return to their communities, often within a year.

As the number of New Yorkers placed in city jails has shrunk, dealing with those who are jailed has become more challenging, corrections officials say. They say a larger share of the population is most likely struggling with mental illnesses, for example. This year, the rate of serious injury to those in custody as a result of violence among inmates rose by nearly 24 percent, and the rate of serious injury to correction officers from assaults by inmates rose by 37 percent, according to the Mayor's Management Report, released last month.

Getting the jail plan approved by the City Council will require additional investments from City Hall in mental health and other services sought by communities surrounding the jails. In a change that should increase support for the plan, city officials said Friday that they had reduced the combined number of beds in the four proposed local jails to 3,795 from about 4,600. The figure includes 15 percent more beds than are likely to be necessary if the most optimistic predictions hold, to account for fluctuations in the jail population. The three existing local facilities have a combined capacity of 2,454 people.

Modern jails can be more humane jails. And it is better for New Yorkers to stay in their communities while legal proceedings are underway, rather than to be shipped to an island in the East River far from family and support networks. "We need to do this work with more compassion, more understanding," said Capt. Justina Corporan, a senior corrections officer, while giving reporters a tour of the aging Rikers complex. "The line that separates the people on the inside from the people on the outside is thinner than anyone thinks."

Glossary

aboriginal Being indigenous to a particular place, typically referring to Australia's first settled populations.

austerity A fiscal policy of reduced spending, typically targeting social welfare.

"broken windows" policing Policing based on the theory that prosecuting smaller crimes helps prevent more serious crimes from occurring.

cash bail A required amount of money offered by a defendant to a court in exchange for release from jail, with that money's return after the trial.

community policing A style of policing that prioritizes building community trust.

criminalization Making an action illegal with new laws.

criminology The scientific study of the causes and effects of crime, as well as methods of combating it.

deterrence The act of discouraging an action, seen as one goal of criminal justice.

disproportionate When an effect on something is measurably greater or less than on something else.

diversionary conferencing A restorative justice practice, whereby an offender and victim enter into a dialogue outside of a formal court system.

mandatory minimums Sentencing laws that establish a minimum sentence for a class of crime, limiting the discretion of a judge.

militarization The process of becoming more prepared and oriented toward violence or conflict, usually by the acquisition of increasingly powerful weapons.

parole The early reduction of a prison sentence, premised on the former convict's good behavior on release.

police commissioner A civilian supervisor of policing, distinct from a police chief in their policy-making role.

property crime A class of crimes focusing on loss or destruction of property, including vandalism, arson, and theft.

punitive A style of criminal justice specifically intended to punish.

rank-and-file Non-leadership status in an organization like a trade union.

recidivism The repeat of a criminal offense by a former offender.

rehabilitation One model for responding to crime, whereby an offender gets resources and training to live without resorting to crime.

restitution The compensation of a harm, loss or theft.

school-to-prison pipeline A pattern where punitive school discipline increases the likelihood of a child entering juvenile detention, and possibly prison.

stop-and-frisk A policing procedure of briefly detaining and frisking citizens, intended as a deterrent to crime.

systemic racism Patterns of harm to racial groups caused by institutions or society, rather than by individuals.

"three-strikes" laws Sentencing laws aimed at reducing crime by giving lengthy or life sentences to offenders committing three felonies or more.

vigilante A person or group granting itself law enforcement powers without the sanction of the law.

war on drugs An American federal policy aimed at reducing illegal drug use, launched in 1971.

Media Literacy Terms

"Media literacy" refers to the ability to access, understand, critically assess and create media. The following terms are important components of media literacy, and they will help you critically engage with the articles in this title.

angle The aspect of a news story that a journalist focuses on and develops.

attribution The method by which a source is identified or by which facts and information are assigned to the person who provided them.

balance Principle of journalism that both perspectives of an argument should be presented in a fair way.

bias A disposition of prejudice in favor of a certain idea, person or perspective.

byline Name of the writer, usually placed between the headline and the story.

chronological order Method of writing a story presenting the details of the story in the order in which they occurred.

credibility The quality of being trustworthy and believable, said of a journalistic source.

editorial Article of opinion or interpretation.

feature story Article designed to entertain as well as to inform.

headline Type, usually 18 point or larger, used to introduce a story.

human interest story Type of story that focuses on individuals and how events or issues affect their life, generally offering a sense of relatability to the reader.

impartiality Principle of journalism that a story should not reflect a journalist's bias and should contain balance.

intention The motive or reason behind something, such as the publication of a news story.

interview story Type of story in which the facts are gathered primarily by interviewing another person or persons.

inverted pyramid Method of writing a story using facts in order of importance, beginning with a lead and then gradually adding paragraphs in order of relevance from most interesting to least interesting.

motive The reason behind something, such as the publication of a news story or a source's perspective on an issue.

news story An article or style of expository writing that reports news, generally in a straightforward fashion and without editorial comment.

op-ed An opinion piece that reflects a prominent individual's opinion on a topic of interest.

paraphrase The summary of an individual's words, with attribution, rather than a direct quotation of their exact words.

quotation The use of an individual's exact words indicated by the use of quotation marks and proper attribution.

reliability The quality of being dependable and accurate, said of a journalistic source.

rhetorical device Technique in writing intending to persuade the reader or communicate a message from a certain perspective.

tone A manner of expression in writing or speech.

Media Literacy Questions

1. "Prison and the Poverty Trap" (on page 20) is an example of a human interest story. What are some of the ways the author personalizes his interview subjects?

2. Bryan Stevenson's article "Why American Prisons Owe Their Cruelty to Slavery" (on page 35) comes from the 1619 Project, an initiative by The New York Times on the legacy of slavery in American life. How does this angle shape the author's analysis?

3. "Bratton Says New York Police Officers Must Fight Bias" (on page 46) combines quotations and paraphrase from a variety of law enforcement sources. Compare one paraphrase with one quote, to determine how the author chose which information needed to be expressed directly.

4. "I'm a Police Chief. We Need to Change How Officers View Their Guns." (on page 67) is an op-ed by a chief of police. What particular point of view does the author provide, and how does a policing background support it?

5. "Blacks Mull Call for 10,000 to Curb Violence" (on page 76) presents conflicting views on a proposed community watch program. How does the author present the rationale behind those views? Does the author remain impartial?

6. In "Attica, Attica: The Story of the Legendary Prison Uprising" (on page 95), the author alludes to a film and a popular song that each reference the Attica uprising. What is the purpose of the rhetorical device of allusion in this article?

7. "Can Forgiveness Play a Role in Criminal Justice?" (on page 108) is a feature story, written in chronological order in a narrative style. Why do you think the author chose to write it this way?

8. What is the tone of the article "Could Restorative Justice Fix the Internet?" (on page 153)? How does the author's writing style contribute to that tone?

9. Some headlines state the subject directly, while other headlines are less direct. Based on the contents of the article "Why Are American Prisons So Afraid of This Book?" (on page 157), what might the style of the headline be trying to convey?

10. "Is Prison Necessary? Ruth Wilson Gilmore Might Change Your Mind" (on page 169) is an interview story. What is the background of the chief subject, Ruth Wilson Gilmore, and how do her statements contribute to the article's reporting on the prison abolition movement?

11. "For Real Community Policing, Let Officers Do Their Jobs" (on page 198) is also an op-ed by a police chief. What point of view does this piece represent? Compare it with "I'm a Police Chief. We Need to Change How Officers View Their Guns." (on page 67).

12. "How to Close Rikers Island" (on page 206) is an editorial by the New York Times editorial board. Based on its overview of conflicting positions on New York's jail system, how does the editorial board explain its core recommendations?

Citations

All citations in this list are formatted according to the Modern Language Association's (MLA) style guide.

BOOK CITATION

THE NEW YORK TIMES EDITORIAL STAFF. *Restorative Justice: An Alternative to Punishment.* New York Times Educational Publishing, 2021.

ONLINE ARTICLE CITATIONS

ALEXANDER, MICHELLE. "Reckoning With Violence." *The New York Times,* 3 Mar. 2019, https://www.nytimes.com/2019/03/03/opinion/violence -criminal-justice.html.

ARCHIBOLD, RANDAL C. "A Quandary for Mexico as Vigilantes Rise." *The New York Times,* 15 Jan. 2014, https://www.nytimes.com/2014/01/16/world /americas/a-quandary-for-mexico-as-vigilantes-rise.html.

BAZELON, EMILY, AND MIRIAM KRINSKY. "There's a Wave of New Prosecutors. And They Mean Justice." *The New York Times,* 11 Dec. 2018, https:// www.nytimes.com/2018/12/11/opinion/how-local-prosecutors-can -reform-their-justice-systems.html.

BEAVERS, ELIZABETH R., AND MICHAEL SHANK. "Get the Military Off of Main Street." *The New York Times,* 14 Aug. 2014, https://www.nytimes .com/2014/08/15/opinion/ferguson-shows-the-risks-of-militarized -policing.html.

BECK, CHARLIE, AND CONNIE RICE. "How Community Policing Can Work." *The New York Times,* 12 Aug. 2016, https://www.nytimes.com/2016/08/12 /opinion/how-community-policing-can-work.html.

BENKO, JESSICA. "The Radical Humaneness of Norway's Halden Prison." *The New York Times,* 26 Mar. 2015, https://www.nytimes.com/2015 /03/29/magazine/the-radical-humaneness-of-norways-halden-prison .html.

BROMWICH, JONAH ENGEL. "Why Are American Prisons So Afraid of This Book?" *The New York Times*, 18 Jan. 2018, https://www.nytimes.com /2018/01/18/us/new-jim-crow-book-ban-prison.html.

BROWN, PATRICIA LEIGH. "Opening Up, Students Transform a Vicious Circle." *The New York Times*, 3 Apr. 2013, https://www.nytimes.com/2013/04/04 /education/restorative-justice-programs-take-root-in-schools.html.

CROMIDAS, RACHEL. "The Pulse: Antiviolence Ritual From a Faraway Land." *The New York Times*, 13 Aug. 2010, https://www.nytimes.com/2010/08/13 /us/13cncpulse_1.html.

DAVEY, MONICA, AND MITCH SMITH. "Chicago Police Department Plagued by Systemic Racism, Task Force Finds." *The New York Times*, 13 Apr. 2016, https://www.nytimes.com/2016/04/14/us/chicago-police-dept-plagued -by-systemic-racism-task-force-finds.html.

DEL POZO, BRANDON. "I'm a Police Chief. We Need to Change How Officers View Their Guns." *The New York Times*, 13 Nov. 2019, https://www .nytimes.com/2019/11/13/opinion/police-shootings-guns.html.

DEWAN, SHAILA. "The Real Murder Mystery? It's the Low Crime Rate." *The New York Times*, 1 Aug. 2009, https://www.nytimes.com/2009/08/02 /weekinreview/02dewan.html.

FARNSWORTH, CLYDE H. "This Penal Colony Learned a Lesson." *The New York Times*, 10 Aug. 1997, https://www.nytimes.com/1997/08/10/weekinreview /this-penal-colony-learned-a-lesson.html.

FORMAN, JAMES, JR. "Attica, Attica: The Story of the Legendary Prison Uprising." *The New York Times*, 30 Aug. 2016, https://www.nytimes .com/2016/09/04/books/review/blood-in-the-water-attica-heather -ann-thompson.html.

FORMAN, JAMES, JR., AND TREVOR STUTZ. "Beyond Stop-and-Frisk." *The New York Times*, 19 Apr. 2012, https://www.nytimes.com/2012/04/20 /opinion/better-ways-to-police-than-stop-and-frisk.html.

FORTIN, JACEY. "California Allows Public to Refuse to Help Law Enforcement." *The New York Times*, 6 Sept. 2019, https://www.nytimes.com/2019/09/06 /us/california-posse-comitatus-act.html.

GOODMAN, J. DAVID. "Bratton Says New York Police Officers Must Fight Bias." *The New York Times*, 24 Feb. 2015, https://www.nytimes.com/2015/02/25 /nyregion/new-yorks-police-commissioner-says-officers-must-fight-bias .html.

GREGORY, KIA. "From Terrorizing Streets to Making Them Safer." *The New*

York Times, 24 Apr. 2013, https://www.nytimes.com/2013/04/25/nyregion /harlem-man-tells-of-escape-from-a-violent-life.html.

HURDLE, JON. "Blacks Mull Call for 10,000 to Curb Violence." *The New York Times*, 30 Sept. 2007, https://www.nytimes.com/2007/09/30/us /30philadelphia.html.

KRAFT, DINA. "By Talking, Inmates and Victims Make Things 'More Right.' " *The New York Times*, 5 July 2014, https://www.nytimes.com/2014/07/06/us /by-talking-inmates-and-victims-make-things-more-right.html.

KUSHNER, RACHEL. "Is Prison Necessary? Ruth Wilson Gilmore Might Change Your Mind." *The New York Times*, 17 Apr. 2019, https://www .nytimes.com/2019/04/17/magazine/prison-abolition-ruth-wilson -gilmore.html.

LIPTAK, ADAM. "U.S. Prison Population Dwarfs That of Other Nations." *The New York Times*, 23 Apr. 2008, https://www.nytimes.com/2008/04/23 /world/americas/23iht-23prison.12253738.html.

LYNCH, PATRICK J. "For Real Community Policing, Let Officers Do Their Jobs." *The New York Times*, 27 Oct. 2016, https://www.nytimes.com/2016/10/27 /opinion/for-real-community-policing-let-officers-do-their-jobs.html.

MEDINA, JENNIFER. "Los Angeles to Reduce Arrest Rate in Schools." *The New York Times*, 18 Aug. 2014, https://www.nytimes.com/2014/08/19/us /los-angeles-to-reduce-arrest-rate-in-schools.html.

THE NEW YORK TIMES. "How to Close Rikers Island." *The New York Times*, 13 Oct. 2019, https://www.nytimes.com/2019/10/13/opinion/rikers -island-closing.html.

SALCEDO, ANDREA. "The Secret Behind the Viral Churro Seller Video." *The New York Times*, 18 Nov. 2019, https://www.nytimes.com/2019/11/18 /nyregion/churro-lady-video-subway.html.

SMITH, MITCH. "Policing: What Changed (and What Didn't) Since Michael Brown Died." *The New York Times*, 7 Aug. 2019, https://www.nytimes .com/2019/08/07/us/racism-ferguson.html.

SMITH, MITCH. "Rahm Emanuel Unveils Changes for Chicago Police but Ignores Much of Panel's Advice." *The New York Times*, 21 Apr. 2016, https://www.nytimes.com/2016/04/22/us/rahm-emanuel-unveils -changes-for-chicago-police-but-ignores-much-of-panels-advice.html.

STEVENSON, BRYAN. "Why American Prisons Owe Their Cruelty to Slavery." *The New York Times*, 14 Aug. 2019, https://www.nytimes.com/interactive /2019/08/14/magazine/prison-industrial-complex-slavery-racism.html.

TIERNEY, JOHN. "Prison and the Poverty Trap." *The New York Times*, 18 Feb. 2013, https://www.nytimes.com/2013/02/19/science/long-prison-terms-eyed-as-contributing-to-poverty.html.

TULLIS, PAUL. "Can Forgiveness Play a Role in Criminal Justice?" *The New York Times*, 4 Jan. 2013, https://www.nytimes.com/2013/01/06/magazine/can-forgiveness-play-a-role-in-criminal-justice.html.

WARZEL, CHARLIE. "Could Restorative Justice Fix the Internet?" *The New York Times*, 20 Aug. 2019, https://www.nytimes.com/2019/08/20/opinion/internet-harassment-restorative-justice.html.

WEGMAN, JESSE. "In the Bronx, New Life for an Old Prison." *The New York Times*, 2 Feb. 2015, https://www.nytimes.com/2015/02/02/opinion/in-the-bronx-new-life-for-an-old-prison.html.

WILLIAMS, TIMOTHY. "Prisons Have Become Warehouses for the Poor, Ill and Addicted, a Report Says." *The New York Times*, 11 Feb. 2015, https://www.nytimes.com/2015/02/11/us/jails-have-become-warehouses-for-the-poor-ill-and-addicted-a-report-says.html.

WILLIAMS, TIMOTHY, AND JOHN ELIGON. "The Lives of Ferguson Activists, Five Years Later." *The New York Times*, 9 Aug. 2019, https://www.nytimes.com/2019/08/09/us/ferguson-activists.html.

Index

This book is current up until the time of printing. For the most up-to-date reporting, visit www.nytimes.com.